The Wrong Side of Midnight

AP Cleriot

Published by AP Cleriot, 2024.

THE WRONG SIDE OF MIDNIGHT

First edition. October 5, 2024.

ISBN: 979-8224568260

Written by AP Cleriot.

Also by AP Cleriot

Collegiate
The Wrong Side of Midnight

Watch for more at https://linktr.ee/cleriotnoir.

This book is dedicated to my wife. She is my partner in life, my soulmate, my Emerald. Thank you for putting up with me.

Foreword

I WAS AT THE END OF my writing life. Cracked.com had switched owners, and things changed drastically all over the internet. While I certainly wasn't making a living from my nonfiction work, I had exposure and an audience. Many of my freelancer friends from Cracked had spun careers from their contributions to the website. The comedic, writing gods I looked up to - Robert Brockway, Dan O'Brien, Jason Pargin, Soren Bowie, and more - all had humble beginnings and are now writing best selling novels and TV shows you've probably watched. But the legendary workshop at Cracked, where these amazing mentors gave their time and advice free of charge, was slipping away. I had less time for pitches, but always thought I'd get back to it someday, and then my writing career would take off too. But the workshop itself closed and the website underwent further changes. The millions of people that used to read articles daily moved on, and my hopes of springboarding to a moderate writing career was lost.

So I tried to give up. I tried so hard not to write. I worked out, taught courses, got other jobs unrelated to my childhood dream.

And I was miserable. Writing had always been my outlet, the way I slipped out of the world, and meditated.

I began to write again. Sent some stories to publications and was soundly rejected each time. I was out of practice and definitely not hip to modern trends.

So again, I gave it up. And again, embraced misery. Some Christmas came along and with it New Years. I looked back at the previous year, and saw how badly I'd spun my tires. What did I want to do? I wanted to write. I wanted to write so badly, but why? I hadn't found an audience for my fiction. Maybe I'd been deluding myself. I sucked. I should give up this stupid obsession.

But sure enough, it started again. Fine, I thought, I'll write because it's therapeutic. I'll write and not do a thing with the stories.

For a time, this approach worked. I wrote a bunch without worrying about reception or quality and had a decent time. I was like a whittler, carving pointy sticks, enjoying the quiet distraction.

The stories turned into a novel, and my wife made a crucial suggestion. If you're writing them, why not publish too? I mentioned the rejections, and she clarified. Just publish them yourself, wherever. They're just sitting there anyway. What did I have to lose?

Nothing, I answered. A lot, I remember thinking. I'm under no delusions of grandeur. In no way am I the greatest writer on the planet. Often I'm only so-so, and occasionally good. But she had a point. I looked for platforms, and tried a few, but only one stood out: NoSleep on reddit.

It's not as popular as it used to be but the readers there are more plentiful than most places, and kind too. I posted a story, and got immediate feedback. It felt amazing to have my work read again. Instantly, I became addicted, and resolved to post work on a weekly basis. Dozens of stories later, over the course of a year, and here we are.

My love of writing is rekindled, and while I won't soon be quitting my day job, I am immensely grateful to bring you this collection of my most well received stories of 2023-2024 (+1 new story)

Whether you are a new reader or one of the NoSleepers who sent me messages of support, thank you. You give me hope.

Sincerely,

AP Cleriot

The Orange Horse

IT COULDN'T BE.

I dropped the reusable bags but kept walking, kicking through the pile on my way into the store.

"Uh, Chris?" Shannon asked. "The bags?"

"Yeah, yeah." I didn't stop, leaving her behind in the lobby. I walked through the produce section to clothing to housewares to a wall of toilet paper. The Value Club had everything but an easily accessible back door.

Shannon found me sitting on a gigantic multipack of triple-ply quilted, the good stuff.

"Hi," I said, afraid to look at her.

"Hi," she said before sitting beside me. The pack was so wide, practically a couch.

"Did you know Value Club is actually the last Price Club and the managers pooled their money to keep it out of the Costco merger?"

"I did," Shannon said. "Someone usually mentions it every single time we shop here." She squeezed my kneecap. "Want to tell me why you're sitting on toilet paper? That's new."

"Can we leave first?"

My wife's dark eyebrows knitted with concern. "Chris, what's going on?"

"We have to go, Shannon," I urged her, panic beginning to rise. "The orange horse," I whispered, "is here." I covered my mouth, afraid that it might hear.

"The what?"

I wrung my hands. "Didn't you see it? It's right inside the front doors. The coin operated ride. Oh god, what if some kid rides it? That's why it's here. Of course. Why else?"

"Chris," Shannon said slowly, "you're scaring me."

"We have to go." I tugged on her wrist.

1

"Okay, okay, we can go." She started pulling me because I only stared helplessly at the toilet paper wall again. "Come on."

"Not that way!" I said too loud. A teen moving paper towels from a pallet to another pallet stopped and took out his earbuds. "We have to go out the back," I said more calmly.

Patiently, Shannon helped us find an exit through a delivery bay. We had to walk around the fortress of a store in the rain. I wouldn't let her go back into the lobby for the bags I'd dropped.

"Chris, come on. It's wasteful."

I'd already started the car. "You should have got them before."

"When *you* dropped them?"

"Yeah."

"I was more worried about my flaky husband."

"Get in the car, Shannon. There's no time." If she went back in, I would have left her behind. I love her but this fear runs deeper. She would have understood if she'd been there all those years ago with the orange horse.

When we were safe(r) in our kitchen and had changed out of our wet clothes, I opened up two bottles of wine and set them on the granite island.

"Gonna be some afternoon," she said, going to the cupboard for our wine glasses. Retreating to the living room couch, Shannon waited patiently while I lit the fireplace and drank and muttered about the heavy rain and whether or not our stunted trees by the back fence could survive another deluge.

Eventually, the alcohol wore through her patience. Shannon was not happy drunk. Neither was she mean, however. Aggressive would be more accurate. Often sexually, which I would have enjoyed if not for that thing at Value Club.

"Spill it, my love," she demanded.

I drained my glass and poured some more.

"Enough dramatics. Now, Chris."

2

"I'm not trying to be dramatic," I said truthfully. "I'm procrastinating because I don't want to talk about it. I don't ever want to think about it. It was thirty years ago."

"Chris..."

"Okay. Okay." I had to work up to it. "Remember Channel 14?"

She shook her head. "Not at all. Channel 14?"

"Local cable," I said. "It ran local TV shows. Pretty much all garbage, created by the best losers of Bridal Veil Lake. Anyone could have a show if they had a bit of money or a connection."

She sipped her wine, readying herself for what I was about to drop. Shannon is the best. Did I really want to bring her into my nightmares? She deserved better. We would stop going to Value Club. A childless couple didn't need to shop there. We just liked big stuff.

I put down my wine.

"Oh no you don't," she said, gripping my forearm, at first tenderly, and then pressing her sharp nails against my skin. "My love, if you don't tell me now, I intend to draw blood." She smiled and I knew the threat would be carried out.

"Okay, okay, so..."

The tip of talons dug in.

I yelped. "A talking horse! A talking horse! I was on a kids' show about a talking horse."

Nails relented, and her touch became comforting again. "The orange horse?"

I nodded. I had to sit down in one of our reading chairs by the fire.

My wife looked worried. I never acted like this. Our decade of marriage had been carefree and easy. "What happened on the show, Chris?"

"The horse could talk."

"Yes, you said that-"

"No, you don't understand. It could really talk. The hard plastic mouth moved and it could talk. The eyes too. The painted black dots rolled around in the whites." I shivered despite the waves of heat coming from the fire.

Shannon topped us up. "You never mentioned being on a kid's show before. How old were you?"

"Four. Five when it ended. I was the last kid. I can't remember the names of the others. One was Bella, I think. It called her Octa-Bella. I don't know why."

"Well, now I have to see, Chris," she said. She took out her phone.

"Good luck finding a copy of that-"

"Your mom has it in the shared drive."

Of course she did.

Shannon started watching with the volume high. Mom, damn it, she never understood the dread of that place, and didn't believe me when I said I was scared. To this day, she thinks we don't speak or see each other often because I'm so busy. The truth is I'll never stop resenting her for bringing me to Channel 14.

I didn't have to see the video on Shannon's phone to pair the awful piano intro with the black screen gradually filled with mechanical white type: The Orange Horse.

The words disappear and then, depending on the episode, there are kids, or one kid, on a stage in the dark, surrounding a shiny orange horse, a coin operated ride with a real leather saddle and reins that never helped anyone.

Poor sound quality picks up or makes an ambient buzzing that persists throughout each episode. That sound makes my stomach turn because it means it will speak soon, and it will choose.

"Hello children," says the orange horse, his voice a deep and unfriendly monotone. "Which one of you will try tonight? Have you decided? Or shall I?" The hinged mouth moves but rarely in synchronization with its words.

As Shannon watched and listened, I recalled the strong oiled scent of the mechanical beast and the way its pinprick eyes could swell until they took away the rest of the already empty scene and you would be alone with it. No one could come to save you, even had they wanted to.

Shannon paused the screen with her thumb. "Hang on, there's a timestamp thingy in the corner. Past midnight. Were you filming at night? That couldn't have been legal. Not even in the 80s."

"We weren't recording," I said, trembling so hard I could barely drink. "It was live. There wasn't a script. No rehearsals. No crew. Just us and the horse."

Shannon knelt down and weaved her fingers with mine. "My love, there must have been some people. Somebody filmed this. Your mom, for all her faults, wouldn't have ditched you with nobody."

"She brought a toddler there at midnight," I said, more angrily than expected. "You overestimate her parenting." Still, Shannon's suggestion stirred up a memory.

There had been an old man, a somber, silent guy. I don't remember him saying anything. He opened the studio doors and ensured they closed behind me.

"Have fun," my mom would say from the walkway outside. Channel 14 was a small, squat building, a brown, windowless rectangle. It'd been on the outskirts of Bridal Veil Lake beside a strip joint that never changed its sign: Grand Opening December.

The old guy would point the way to the heavy curtain at the end of a long, dim hallway. None of the track lights above were ever completely functional. They flickered and held on to burnt out tubes that seemed to emit a smoke coiling around the popcorn ceiling.

Beyond the curtain, the other kids were already there. We never talked or said hello. The orange horse ride waited, a presence demanding your attention. I remember the kids screaming when it spoke.

If you hadn't been through the ordeal already, you screamed. Some weeks there were a lot that screamed. Most times we waited for it to choose a rider in silence.

Often, the heavy oil odour would turn my stomach. There was another little girl in a knitted, pink sweater. She used to hold my hand until the night she was chosen. I never saw her again after that.

I remember her ride.

I remember prying my fingers from hers, and how she cried when the orange horse said her name. Stirrups, a rein, and the pommel were all too big for children. The saddle had been made with adults in mind it seemed.

"Erin, it's your turn to ride, time to see what wriggles inside." Its rhyme was as clumsy as its mouth. The eyes rolled and stopped with a sharp click that always made the chosen rider flinch. They were just dots of paint, and yet you just knew when the orange horse stared at you.

Her little hand slipped on the hard plastic mane as she tried to climb up. I steadied her and helped her on. She wrapped the reins around her forearms. The stirrups were too low; she couldn't put her feet through, so she tried to brace her heels against the lump of tail fused to the orange body. Others had tried that too.

The ride started gently at first, and then, without warning...

"Chris! Chris!" Shannon was shouting at me. A frantic shrieking tore from my throat. I lay on the floor by the fireplace and the waves of heat were too much. Sweat and drool and tears ran in rivulets down my face and body. I'd also pissed myself but didn't notice until I got changed later.

My wife held me without judgment and rocked me back and forth as she did when this would happen in the middle of the night.

"Oh my god, it's your night terrors," she said. "This is what they're about."

"Yeah," I admitted weakly. "Did you see it? Did you see what it did?"

She shook her head. "The ride starts and the footage ends immediately. You were so cute, but, yeah, not happy. None of the kids looked very happy."

"We weren't."

Shannon tapped her phone and brought it to her ear.

"What are you doing?"

"Calling your mom," she said.

"What? Why?" I tried to get up and found that more difficult than expected due to drunkenness and wobbly limbs full of fear.

"Hey, Jacqueline, yeah, it's Shannon." She walked off and I heard the side door swing open and bang shut. Her voice became an angry murmur through the walls. Not a nice drinker at all.

I sprawled on the couch and watched the fire.

The side door banged again and Shannon stood above me. "Let's go." She took my hand and started pulling.

"What? Where?" I was afraid I already knew.

"To that stupid horse ride."

I leaned back, and she groaned from the sudden extra weight. "Come on, Chris. You need to see that it's just a toy, and nothing-"

"It's not, it's not. I'm not going back. We're never going there again."

"Chris, sweetheart," she said with false patience, "your mom explained it all. T

You wanted to be on the show because you watched it on TV. She thought it'd be a good way for you to meet some other kids. When it was canceled, she said you were sad."

"And you believed her?" I wrung my hand out of Shannon's. "What about all the kids?"

"What about them?"

"They didn't come back..." I tried to remember Erin's ride and what had happened. The orange horse always got carried away and the kids fell off, and then... I couldn't remember.

"So you think the orange horse killed them? And your mom thought that was great and kept bringing you? Chris, be reasonable. There's no mention of this show on the internet, and nothing about kids dying on a show or going missing. Was it a weird experience?

For sure. Did it traumatize you? Yes. Was a plastic horse somehow responsible or were you just so young that your mind misinterpreted details, got confused, and made it scarier than it seemed?"

"Shannon," I said, weary from her rant. "You weren't there."

"True, but where was I when I was four? I couldn't tell you. We barely remember anything before five. And what we do recall can be easily misconstrued due to our underdeveloped kid brains."

She was beginning to make sense, and I started to feel a little dumb. The fear remained, however, and I didn't want to go to Value Club. We argued some more, and came to a compromise by evening: Baby steps.

We'd pay the orange horse a quick visit after supper, and I could say when it was time to leave. The store didn't close until nine. Since we were a little drunk, we'd take a taxi. It all seemed so reasonable.

I hesitated outside the automatic sliding doors. A steady stream of customers gave us looks, some irritated, as they passed around Shannon and I. She tugged gently on my arm and whispered support.

Every instinct told me to run. That thing waited inside, just on the other side of some opaque glass. I held my breath, closed my eyes, and let her be my guide. The oiled saddle clotted the air with its odour. I gasped because I thought we were close to it.

When I opened my eyes, the stench seemed to fade, and the orange horse was still some meters away. Its long body gleamed beneath the huge lights hanging from the ceiling. I could see our faint shadows in its hind quarters.

"You okay, Chris?" Shannon asked. "You want to go?"

I kept staring at the horse's face. The pinpoint eyes were needles. The closed mouth hid teeth. There were teeth in there. Surely, that hadn't been a false memory.

"Chris?"

"Do you have a quarter?"

She opened her hand, the warm coin inside. "You don't have to. Really, I'm sorry if I was pushy. Clearly, this thing freaked you out a lot when you were a kid. Imagine how tired you must have been, filming at midnight."

I remembered the last show.

"Christopher," it said, "it's your time to ride, time to see what wriggles inside." Five-years-old and I felt a hundred. I was the last one, the only kid on the stage that night.

The orange horse had no one but me to choose. So I started climbing up to the saddle before its clunky mouth shut.

But then...

"I slipped off," I told Shannon.

"You what?" She'd been staring at the orange horse too, and had her arms wrapped around herself. "This thing is sort of creepy. No wonder you're traumatized. Gotta be worse in the dark, alone."

"When it was my turn," I said, "there was no one there to catch me when I lost my grip on the stupid mane. I fell and cut my lip, I think. Somebody came and brought me outside to my mom. She was smoking and sitting on the hood of our car. My lip got so fat."

"Why were you alone?"

"I don't know."

"Are you sure you *were* alone, Chris?" Shannon asked reluctantly. "I mean, it doesn't make a lot of sense. We should talk to your mom again. I shouldn't have yelled at her."

I looked at the quarter. The orange horse worked on its own. It moved without money. I tried hard to recall a coin slot, but couldn't.

Doubt gnawed hard at my certainty about the stupid ride and the whole Channel 14 ordeal. Maybe the ride just looked like the one from my memory. Yet, I'd started trembling so much, I dropped the quarter.

That's when its mouth unhinged to reveal paint chipped squares resembling teeth, and the eyeballs rotated around and around.

I seized hold of Shannon as she put a protective arm in front of me.

A speaker somewhere inside the horse began a script so static ridden we couldn't make out any words.

"Okay, that is scary," Shannon confirmed. I backed away from her and the orange horse. "Chris?"

"I want to leave now. You said I could decide. I'm deciding. Let's go. Please, Shannon, please. I want to go." The voice had been incomprehensible but I felt called to ride. I'd never done mine. Only I had escaped. What had happened to the other kids?

Time to see what wriggles inside...

"Fuck this thing," Shannon said. She scooped up the quarter and advanced on the ride. I swear its attention shifted from me, and I felt so guilty, but the sense of relief wasn't mere imagination.

"Shannon," I said, "get away from it." I wanted to go closer and pull her away, but couldn't get my legs to move. "Shannon..."

She swung her long leg over the saddle and picked up the reins. "This is the most poorly thought out children's ride ever. Her feet slid into the stirrups easily because the whole saddle had, of course, been originally made for an adult. The orange horse looked small beneath her. "You're going to see, Chris. I'm going to show you."

"Shannon, don't-"

Her whole body jolted intensely after the first sway of the ride. The metal in the stirrup made contact with the steel base, where an exposed wire coiled below in the interior, electrifying the plate into an instrument of death.

She didn't look dead. I smelled her death - her cooking flesh - before I saw it.

Had I not been a coward, and tried to grab her, I'd have been electrocuted too.

Employees raced around and an old guy used a broom to unplug the ride. Shannon's body slumped over the orange horse as its eyes spun around one last time.

It's your turn to ride...

I could hear its voice so perfectly within my thoughts.

"It's happened before," my mom said, "in China. I looked it up." We were suddenly sitting inside an ambulance and I don't remember when she arrived or how we got here." My eyes felt sore. "Kids never could reach the stirrups, and even then, it was a fluke, Chris. If the steel part hadn't touched the other steel part, well, we wouldn't..." She cleared her throat, unable to finish her sentence.

"Mom," I said, "why did you put me on that show?"

"The show? Channel 14?" She pretended to clear her throat again. "You were fascinated with the horse. You begged me to take you to see it, even when they weren't filming. Even when there were no other kids there. You loved that thing."

"I didn't," I said. "It scared me. What was the show about?"

"The orange horse," she said, as if that explained it all. A paramedic appeared to check on me. The ambulance started moving. We were going to the hospital.

Time launched itself to Shannon's funeral and then an idle Tuesday afternoon of no particular importance. I held another glass of wine. I sat in one of the reading chairs. Hers remained empty.

Would always be empty.

Heavy rain poured. Those stunted trees by the fence were up to their evergreens in water.

It was just an accident. My mom had been right about coin operated rides. Apparently, they send kids to hospitals every year. Even the exposed wire thing had happened before.

I started to cry. If I hadn't gotten so spooked in Value Club, Shannon would be here, alive, and we'd be happy.

"Stupid horse," I cursed into my cup before slurping some more wine.

That's when the TV came on. It began with a warm, yellow light in the center of the screen, which expanded until the typewriter noise began. I seized the arms of the chair. My cup shattered against the fireplace.

THEORANGEHORSE

The white letters appeared one at a time with the mashing of those keys. A blurry scene gradually focused like a dream and there I was, five-years-old, exhaustedly standing by the ride.

"Christopher," the horse said, eyes spinning, lazy mouth opening only once for multiple syllables, "it's your turn to ride, time to see what wriggles inside."

I started screaming. My memory hadn't been mistaken about the smallest detail. I had been alone. My small hand reached for the mane and I slipped, and my chin clipped the hard plastic. What happened next, I did not recall.

Five-year-old me sprawled out on the floor. I looked unconscious.

The orange horse snorted and his eyes spun so fast, the black dot blurred into a ragged circle.

"Time to see what wriggles inside," it said again. And then again. And again. And again. I hadn't moved. I was unconscious.

A curtain pushed aside briefly, revealing a host of people sitting on bleachers. I'd always thought we were alone. An older man stepped onto the sound stage and knelt down by my head.

"Kid didn't even make it to the saddle," he called back to the audience and the crowd beyond the curtain laughed until the orange horse emitted a sharp, piercing whinny. They quieted instantly. The older man's smile fell and he bowed his head low, mumbling apologetically as he scooped me up.

The thrum of the lights or a furnace dominated the empty space once more.

"Better take him, Jacks," he said.

The curtain swept aside and my fucking mom walked out in a huff. She had the old guy carry me off the stage. That's about when I started to regain consciousness.

My TV shut off then. It didn't have to show me what followed because I remembered my mom lighting up a cigarette and sitting on the hood of our car.

I must have been groggy from the fall or the late hour. Seemed like we were outside Channel 14 a long time before she took me home. She never said a word. She didn't have to in order to convey her disappointment.

Behind a row of empty bottles, I found my phone. I got my coat and hopped in the car without waiting for a response. She'd be there. I knew she would.

Jacqueline waited inside the front entrance of Value Club, staring at the horse nobody had bothered to move. Only a stretched out bit of caution tape deterred any future riders.

The urge to punch my mom in the back of the head dwindled swiftly in the presence of the orange horse. I felt exhausted and stupid.

"What the fuck, mom?"

"Watch your language, Chris." My mom swore all the time, casually and for fun. Now in her seventies, she rarely hesitated to pepper her judgments of other drivers with a litany of expletives. Her sudden attention to etiquette implied the religious significance of the horse I now suspected.

"So what? You think it's Jesus? Horse Jesus? Fucking plastic horse Jesus?"

"Sh!" she hissed.

The mouth unhinged and popped so hard I thought it would fall off. Again, static came from the deeply buried recorder within. It didn't matter. I knew the words and what it wanted. Unbelievably, the ride remained plugged into the wall, and I had zero confidence the exposed wire had been fixed.

"You never did take your ride, Chris," Jacqueline said. She kept her hands folded against her chest and continued looking at the stupid, fucking horse.

13

"You want me to fucking die? Like the other kids on the show? Fuck, why was it a show? Why did it want a show? Huh?!" I ripped away the caution tape. "Why'd you make it a show, you fucking piece of shit!" I threw an ill advised punch against the side of its head and immediately broke my hand. "Fuck!"

"Christopher!" Jacqueline cradled my swelling, bleeding fist. "The show was an invitation. How was anyone to know about it otherwise? And nobody died. Sure, some kids fell off, and got injured. Most kids, I guess. Nobody died until... Shannon. And that was an accident. The orange horse was a test. If you could hang on, then you were in. If not, then-"

"You were outside. Holy... mom, what the hell is going on? What is this thing?"

She wrapped my hand in a kerchief from her purse and patted my cheek before she spoke. "It's something, Chris. It's really something. That's all I can say with any certainty. The people in this town, they all follow something, and this... this is just the something that found us first. You want to know what it is, then you know what you have to do."

It's your turn to ride.

I started my approach, each step a triumph over fear so deeply ingrained into my character I didn't know myself without it. If I could take that ride, and hang on for the duration, I would be someone totally new.

Shannon's death had been an accident.

Something greater resided in or around the orange horse.

My whole life I'd been waiting to find...

what wriggles inside

I threw up all over the saddle as soon as my undamaged hand gripped the pommel. A strong grip snagged my collar and dragged me away before I could even try to mount. The struggle against the intervener lasted only a few seconds before I was pinned to the ground by three Value Club employees and a security guard.

"Sir! That isn't safe!" the guard yelled in my face.

"Hey," another employee said, "somebody plugged it back in."

Jacqueline was already long gone by that point. Eventually, I calmed down enough to be escorted from the store. My mom wasn't in the parking lot, and she wouldn't answer my calls or texts. Her apartment had been vacated already for a week.

In short, I don't know where she is. Or why she probably wanted me dead.

I got rid of my TV. I'm tempted to ditch all screens, including the one I'm currently typing this on. I'm terrified the orange horse will take it over to send me another video.

Value Club removed the ride. Some PR person promised it'd be destroyed asap. Yet, I got a weird feeling they were lying. I'd chop and burn the evil thing myself if I thought it would kill it.

But the orange horse remains. It visits during my sleep. I'm a kid again, and I always take my ride, and fall off when it gets out of control.

I fall and fall and fall, back into my body, asleep until impact. I sit up and gasp, but my wife isn't there.

Shannon's gone.

And I'm alone because I couldn't ride a stupid, plastic horse.

The First Time I Can Remember

MY MOM FELL DOWN THE stairs and into a laundry basket, where she shrank. She wasn't my mom anymore after that.

I was five, and she didn't fall.

Some people came and took her away. Cops or doctors, I guess.

I went to live with an old lady in a dirty house decorated with discarded cigarette butts and painted walls of nicotine. She occupied the living room in a cloud of second hand neglect and made me call her grandma.

The upstairs basement - better known to non-children as the attic - was the only place in the house that didn't stink. I'd steal a package of bologna from the fridge and flee Grandma's wrath.

I wasn't allowed in the kitchen. She never forgot to feed me because she never remembered in the first place. Whining about it had earned me a whack across the wrist from her cane.

The bologna escape plan had been refined to procedure:

Up the stairs to my room; into the closet where an old dresser had been shoved; climb on dresser; jump up into the open attic panel and grab ahold of the floor edge above; pull self up; slide attic panel back over the access point; listen to Grandma clomp and shout and eventually quit looking for you; eat bologna in the dark.

I'd stored other food up here too, cookies and crackers and quickly learned I wasn't the only one living in the attic. Mice would chew through anything and didn't ask before moving into the pillow I'd stolen from Grandma's bed. It was like Cinderella but with poop everywhere.

The day I found a flashlight beside the bologna in the fridge is the day I cried for my mother. I couldn't quite remember what she looked like. The vague features of her face were permanently etched with paranoia. She was afraid of monsters. That's what I thought. I remember praying they'd leave her alone.

As I stared at the end of the light beam, I recalled clearly her fall down the stairs. Her heels slid over the edge of the carpeted steps. She landed in a crouch in the laundry basket. The shrinking was subtle, minor even.

Her tongue fell out of her wide open mouth like she'd bitten it during the fall. She looked up at me intensely and then, it seemed, not at all as if the capacity to be worried had been exceeded.

The last embers of her fire were extinguished, and she ceased to be my mother because she wasn't anyone after that. Somehow, her mind had been reduced to a blank slate.

I blamed myself. I cried until I fell asleep on the baby mattress I'd dragged into the attic. The flashlight was still on when I awoke. Mice were trying to approach my food pile. They crawled in irregular spurts, imitating dead leaves blowing across the ground, and would suddenly squeak and run away when they got too close.

The flashlight revealed a line of soot drawn around the food. I don't remember organizing the supplies; I may have. But I know I didn't make that circle. Had it been there the whole time? And why were the mice afraid to cross it?

Naturally, I put everything mice might eat or poop on inside the dark circle. I lived by the flashlight and only left the attic to use the bathroom and shower when Grandma would take her weekly trip to the grocery store. On one such excursion, I heard her complaining about a large icicle that had formed on the eavestrough.

"Sure as hell it could kill a fool!" she shouted at someone outside. She grumbled more about the city not helping the elderly enough. I went outside for the first time in many days to see it. Cruel and indifferent as Grandma was, she was not exaggerating about the icicle. In my head, I thought it resembled a large knife. A knificle.

Judging by its position on the eavestrough, it grew right outside a window where I lived in the attic. I'd never noticed a shuttered window before but immediately ran inside to check.

Sure enough, it was there, above my reach, at the opposite end of the attic where I'd made camp. There were boxes of Christmas decorations and more clutter than I'd guessed. I found a chair to stand on and struggled to turn the slats, which had been painted over several times.

I pushed too hard and my slender arm destroyed a section of rotting wood. My hand plunged beyond. My fingers wrapped around, instinctively, the knificle. The ice was smooth and I could sense its weight and destructive potential.

If it didn't stab when it fell, it would still crush an individual below. I retracted my arm and looked outside through the hole and at the hilt of the knificle. I felt armed, powerful, and ashamed. Grandma was messed up, confused, but she didn't deserve to die.

Even a six-year-old could understand that. I climbed down from the chair and saw that daylight had been admitted through the broken slat. I turned off the flashlight until nightfall.

A scream woke me up. Grandma was shouting, swearing, and breaking things on the first floor. The attic seemed to vibrate from the severe impacts below. I held my breath and listened.

"You think you can hide?!" she roared, punctuating the question with the sound of shattering glass. The rest of her tirade couldn't breach the second floor.

The ranting and the destruction seemed to last hours but concluded with a more unsettling quiet. I didn't know what it'd been about or what the final outcome had been. I kept still on the baby mattress until dawn where I finally risked peeing into a metal pale I'd found in the attic.

I heard Grandma's car start and pull away. Time for a wash and a kitchen raid. Lowering the pee bucket onto the dresser first, I then dropped beside it as quietly as a cat. I used a wet cloth on my face and pits and drank as much water as I could handle from the tap.

I stopped at the top of the stairs to view an intense fog of cigarette smoke. It filled the entire first floor, which didn't strike me as impossible at the time. My simple mind thought Grandma's smoke hadn't disappeared because the windows and doors were always closed. It was winter. The smoke couldn't get out.

The picture frames had been knocked off the walls, shattered glass piled at the bottom. I wasn't wearing shoes, so I leapt over the shards and stayed low when I landed and listened: Nothing.

I moved swiftly into the kitchen, noting the overturned table and broken lamp in the hall. The living room door stood open, which was rare. Grandma liked her privacy. I don't know why I didn't just stay focused on the fridge. Crossing the antique threshold of her favored space felt like I'd breached the lair of a dragon. The nicotine stench stung my nostrils and burned my eyes. An electric fireplace from the 70s switched between two fake flames, while a vent pumped too much heat. I began to sweat.

The TV played a soap opera to an empty reclining chair and a plastic covered couch. A small pile of tobacco and rolling papers looked to have been abandoned abruptly. Yet there was no other sign of vandalism like in the rest of the house. Something or someone had drawn her from here perhaps.

Since I couldn't see anything worthwhile to take, I left, slowly. Something didn't feel right.

I closed the door, forgetting it had been open. When I reached for the handle to set it right, it turned on its own. I backed away. She hadn't been inside. No one had. Nevertheless, the door opened outward, and there she stood.

It's difficult to recall exactly her appearance. I remember teeth decayed nearly to the gums, and the wet interior of her mouth a stark contrast to the dry, powdery skin on her wrinkled face. Her dark eyes were so sunken into aged flesh they looked like a shark's.

What she wore and the state of her body I don't remember. She seemed neither fat nor thin. It's the face that remains the clearest . That and the fact she could walk.

The tip of her cane jabbed my baby toe and I hopped back. She pushed open the door and swung, the cane shaft running across the top of my hair. I ran for the stairs.

"Get back here!" she demanded. I made the mistake of glancing over my shoulder as I rounded the bannister, and stepped right onto the broken glass I'd carefully avoided before. Pain shot through the arch of my foot, and my sock turned red.

Grandma's rough arm wrapped around my neck and I suddenly couldn't breathe. Despite her age, her strength exceeded mine by a lot. My small hands slapped ineffectually at her.

She breathed hot, fetid breath into my ear as she spoke. "Don't you see? You're going to die here." The pressure on my neck intensified. I was about to pass out. But somehow - I think she must have adjusted her chokehold - my chin slipped below her forearm. I didn't want to die. Without hesitation, I sank my teeth into her skin until blood filled my mouth, and she finally let go.

This time I didn't look back. I ran up the stairs, ignoring the pain in my foot. There was so much blood, I slipped on the dresser leading to the attic. Grandma switched on the bedroom light as she stomped into the room. We exchanged the briefest look before she rushed for the closet. Her hand closed around my injured foot as I pulled myself up. The blood gushing from the wound saved me. Her fingers slid down my calf to my sock, which came off easily.

I put the panel over the access and sat on it. She pecked with her cane but gave up fast.

"Let it be your tomb then," she seethed before clomping away. I reached the baby mattress with my foot and pulled it over the panel. Then I piled everything I could find except the food, which I left in the black soot circle.

Your foot. Don't forget your foot.

It was like someone had whispered the advice directly to my brain. The wound kept bleeding and I felt sick. I started to panic and cry and desperately wished my mom would save me.

Don't cry. You're going to be okay. Take the blanket and wrap it around the cut.

Except for the first suggestion, I did as recommended.

Now press your hands down on the blanket.

It hurt to do so but I did it and soon the bleeding stopped, and so too my tears.

Listen. That woman is bad. She intends to kill you.

Panic seized my body again.

Listen!

A kind of jolt went through me.

When you hear her car again, go to the window and put your hand against the icicle.

"Knificle?" I said, and I had the strangest feeling whatever was speaking to me smiled.

What a creative, smart child.

I beamed. Then, the sound of Grandma's car came from outside.

Hurry.

It wasn't easy to walk or climb the chair with my hurt foot. The knificle felt wet in the afternoon sun.

Wait.

The nagging feeling I'd had before - that something wasn't the way it should be - came again.

"Something is wrong," I said. My child's brain struggled to connect the scattered details. The engine quieted. A car door slammed shut. Periodic squeaking followed once, twice, three times, and there was grunting from some kind of effort.

Grandma was struggling to do something.

One more second.

"No. I don't want to." I began to retract my arm.

You will die. Do you understand? She intends for you to die. You have no choice. Do you want to die?!

I did not. My hand felt the base of the knificle.

Push. Now.

The base of the large icicle came away from the eavestrough so quietly, so easily. Sour acid filled my stomach.

A soft impact preceded the clattering of steel on wood and concrete. She let out a dismayed cry for help soon after.

I pulled my arm in and looked out at the empty sky while she continued to wail.

I climbed down off the chair and moved quickly to the panel, tossing my junk and the mattress aside.

Where are you going?

"Something isn't right." I couldn't express the obvious any better.

No. Don't go.

I ignored the voice and found my way to the front porch. My remaining sock drank in the wet snow. The wound on my foot felt better against the cold surface.

An old woman lay beside her overturned wheelchair at the bottom of a ramp. Blood matted her white hair. Her teeth weren't rotted; they were white, dentures probably. A package of bologna and a box of cookies lay beside her, and batteries for my flashlight too.

"Are you okay?" she asked. "Did you see that? Big icicle hit me in the head." She tried and failed to get up to a seated position.

"Knificle," I said.

"Huh?" Her eyes scanned the eavestrough where the icicle had been. She saw the hole in the window slat and looked back at me with a worried face. The realization of my betrayal, unintentional as it was, hit us both at the same time. That's when she "shrank."

I learned then what had really happened to my mother the day she fell down the stairs: Nothing. Not to her. It happened to me.

I rose into the air, but it didn't feel like I was being lifted. The subtle decrease in Grandma's size - and my mother's in the past - was my own perception getting further away. The fear, the worry, leaked from her expression; this was beyond her ability to remedy. She wasn't my Grandma anymore.

On a backward trajectory, I floated into the house, carried by something I didn't understand then, and don't fully understand now. I only know when the door slammed shut, I began to resist.

Stop it.

I writhed against the air. "No!"

Stop it. I can help you. I protected you from her. Grandma wanted to hurt you. Kill you.

The whispers in my head became a discordant choir of suffering people. Whatever entity forced their voices into singularity was losing control.

"That wasn't Grandma." I finally understood. "You are!"

I dropped to the floor, free, for the moment. I drew in a big breath and noticed the change in the house immediately. The nicotine coating had lifted, the odour gone. Daylight poured through windows I hadn't noticed before. There was no door barring the living room, which also appeared more inviting. The electric fireplace was gone, and the television was modern, flat, and hung on the wall. Also, it was off.

The destructive debris from earlier was missing too, except for the shards of glass in front of the stairs. I was confused and seemed to drift to my room automatically. Getting the door open, however, proved difficult. Something blocked the way, allowing only what proved to be a me sized gap for my admittance.

Inside the bedroom lay the encampment I thought I'd made in the attic. The mattress was a twin with bedding and a pillow. I had apparently removed it from the bedframe. There were spots of blood on the carpet, which made me remember my foot. The fact I'd forgotten tipped me off to the reduced severity of the wound. There was a cut, and my sock was still missing, but it wasn't gushing blood and probably never had been.

The food pile was in a corner, confined in the black circle. I touched what had been soot; it was wax from crayons.

Only one place left to check. I climbed the dresser in the closet, and found it more difficult to ascend into the attic than expected. When I'd managed to catch the lip of the floor above, my fingers brushed fuzz.

A dead mouse - deceased for some time - lay silent near the opening. The chair beneath the window was, to my disappointment, the same. I had almost killed that old lady. She'd bought me bologna and cookies and other food. I sat down and cried until a man in a uniform came up to collect me.

I was brought to a social worker who had a lot of questions, and wanted to know what had happened. She listened and wrote on a notepad and when I'd finished she gently corrected me on a number of subjects.

I was not six but eight.

The old woman really was my grandma.

I'd lived with her for years already.

She'd been instructed to give me space.

My mother had not been well.

Apparently, neither was I.

My grandmother recovered and welcomed me back in, though she seemed distant and understandably cautious. I attended therapy and progressed well. I went to school, made friends, and usually believed the previous incident had been due to repressed trauma.

Only the empty space where the picture frame had been and my missing sock nagged at me. I hadn't imagined those things. My therapist suggested I'd simply misinterpreted ordinary events.

And I might have accepted that explanation if not for the occasional and fierce sensation that all was still not well.

This feeling would be validated years later, when the memory of these days were firmly rationalized and sealed with medication. The entity tried again.

But even that incident wouldn't be the one to kick off my investigation into Bridal Veil Lake.

That couldn't begin until I understood that evil really does exist. It isn't a metaphor or some subjective truth. It's real and begins with them. Call them demons if you like, though it's probably an oversimplification. Some see themselves as angels, and the rest don't bother to define what they are because they simply don't care.

I won't be upset if you don't believe me. I couldn't accept it until one of them targeted someone else. Someone better than me. Someone I loved, and always will love, wherever they are right now. I hope they are relatively safe in a world where no one ever can be.

This Door Must Remain Closed

MANNEQUIN HEADS GREETED us in the dark. Someone had taken them from the cosmetology class and lined them up across the hallway to be funny and creepy. It worked. The electricity had already been cut off and we'd only one flashlight between the four of us.

I already didn't feel good about breaking into the middle school. The idea that others had already come and messed around made it worse. For Josh, it simply meant there'd be less things to destroy.

And he wanted to destroy it all. To see it, take it in his hands, and then crush it into how he felt. Lakeside Middle School had not been good to any of us, but it'd been especially bad for him and his family.

His older brother, Mark, had just started grade eight when he went missing, never to be seen again. Nasty, baseless rumours circulated that Josh's father had done something and been behind the disappearance. Josh was in grade six then. His mother lost her will to live and simply left town one day. His dad became distant, a silent pariah isolated from the community.

We'd only gone along with the school break-in because Josh wouldn't let it go, and we always felt sorry for him. He looked crazy when he told us they were shutting down the school due to mould and asbestos. Too expensive to fix. Better to let the school die, and the nearby forest swallow it, which it would in about fifty years. Fifty years from 1963.

He acted as if he'd been waiting for this news a long time. We were sixteen, and in high school. There were better ways to spend our nights. Nobody could say no to Josh for long, however. He and his pain were indistinguishable, a constant reminder he'd lost what we took for granted: A loving family.

I kicked through the mannequin heads and Josh stomped one flat. Fred and Rex did it too but their hearts weren't in it. The break-in bored them. They weren't scared of getting in trouble like I was. I wanted to go home.

"Let's go to Bolt's class," Fred said. "See if he left anything behind." He made the drinky-drinky gesture in the dark. Nobody laughed because Lakeview had never been a place of joy. Every locker and alcove passed held memories of hidden assaults on our fragile self-esteem and bodies.

Buried secrets we'd never shared; we thought it was our fault. A kid named Todd held a knife behind my ear in the bathroom while I peed and I thought I'd done something to deserve it.

"Yeah, a drink might help," Rex stated matter-factly. He itched his forearms. Dust and mould clung to the beads of sweat standing out on our skin. There seemed to be a lack of oxygen inside the building. Outside was the cool of early October, and I longed to breathe that fresh air.

Here I held my breath. Not only because of the filth in the interior; I would hold my breath too when moving through these halls when I was a student. Breathing seemed too loud in the austere setting, an oppressive calm full of stoic expectations and suppressed humanity.

Artwork from students was never posted on the walls, which remained bare except for faded photos of humourless classes and staff. We faced a camera like we were in a massive mugshot. Black and white misery, year after year. Not one group held a genuine smile. Not one.

The music classroom, Mr. Bolton's or Bolt's as he was known long before we ever got there, had been barricaded with chairs and already rusted instruments. Impatient about something - maybe his friends - Josh rammed his shoulder against the door until we could slip through.

Someone had set up a camp inside, a squatter who had since departed, though the school had only just been set to close a month ago. It'd been a functioning school prior to the summer. That meant it'd been empty for three months tops. How could so much decay and chaos spread in so little time?

There were plenty of empty bottles around a sleeping bag and Fred despaired until he dug around Bolt's desk and found a large flask full of spoiled red wine. We all took turns forcing down the drink until the nausea in our guts became suppressed by the alcohol.

"Now," Josh said, "Can we please move on?"

"Where?" I asked.

. . . .

"THE DOOR," JOSH SNAPPED and stalked to the door. He had the flashlight. It was follow or be left in the dark. Even buzzed, nobody desired the latter option. We assumed the squatter had left but there was as much chance they'd hid when Josh started ramming the barricade. They'd have to be insane to sleep inside such a gross and miserable place.

"What door?" I asked Josh once we'd finally caught up to the frantic beam of light. He wasn't even using it to see.

"The basement," he said. "This door must remain shut." All of us but him stopped walking. Josh rounded on us and shifted the end of the flashlight from one face to the next. "Why else did you think we were here?"

I shrugged, even more uncomfortable. We'd forgotten about the basement door and Josh's obsession with it. Probably because he hadn't shared it with us until we were about to graduate into high school, a little over two years prior to this moment. He hadn't talked about it in grade nine or ten. The summer between middle and high school had been about nothing else. We forgot about it. He, apparently, did not.

Josh had blamed the middle school for Mark's disappearance. He'd told anyone that would listen that his brother had walked with him to Lakeview on the day he'd gone missing. The school, however, said Mark did not show up to class. His teacher, Mrs. Shipman, marked him absent and swore she never saw him.

So Josh had a theory: Mark had been taken somewhere between the front doors of the school and his class. The ideal location to make him disappear was the basement door near the library. This Door Must Remain Shut it said in big painted letters. I never saw it open. Neither had Fred or Rex, or Josh for that matter.

"You think you'll find something?" Rex asked, the calmest and most resolved of our group. He was often our silent leader because of his detachment. He rested a hand on Josh's shoulder. "Okay, let's check it out."

My guts did a somersault; I blamed the spoiled wine.

Through the dark, down some steps to a landing, and we were already there, faster than I liked. The narrow, worn down stairs suggested frequent passage to and from the door that nobody was supposed to open.

Josh didn't hesitate. He tried the knob first. Locked. He handed me the flashlight, and I held the beam over the railing, a safe distance away and with two exit strategies: Back the way we'd come or to the right, to another set of steps leading to the main floor and the front entrance of the school.

He started kicking the side of the knob, and became more furious when it didn't produce the desired result.

"Josh, we should go," I said. I didn't like all the noise he was making. It was a big school, and we'd seen maybe a third of it since breaking in. Plenty of spots for someone to be. The mannequin heads and the campsite said there were likely squatters around, and who knew if they were friendly? Maybe they were criminals. Psychopathic murderers hiding from eyes, and eager to kill stupid kids who might reveal their location to police.

The knob bent and hung by a single screw. Josh began to yell and curse as he attacked it with even greater rage.

"Josh," Rex said calmly, taking the first step down the stairwell. The way Josh looked at him - like a man possessed - made us all back away.

"The light, goddammit! Bring back the light!" Josh roared at me. I was about to when voices from above, somewhere on the main floor, could be heard. I heard the door knob fall and thunk against the rusted drain on the landing where Josh continued his siege of the basement.

"Someone's there, Josh," Fred said. "Time to leave."

"The light!" Josh commanded again. I've never heard someone yell so loud. It was pleading and promising together. He needed me. There would be consequences for disobedience.

But then steps started shuffling down from above.

"Josh," I called once more, shining the beam on him, just in time to see his shoulder breach the door into the perfect dark beyond.

He squinted up at me. "Come on," I said. But he said it too with his pained expression. Then we went our separate ways: He went into the basement and the rest of us ran from whomever was coming down the steps to the window we'd broken to get inside.

"The light!" I thought I heard him call again from afar.

The three of us fled into the forest and turned off the flashlight and didn't dare to talk. We could see a police car outside the main entrance and then, a few minutes later, the constables themselves were leaving the school.

They didn't have Josh, so we figured he hid and would be out shortly. He was not. It was getting very late and we worried what our parents might do.

"I have to get home," I said to Rex and Fred.

They didn't say what I was thinking: We should go back in and find our friend. Instead, they became complicit and we walked back to our neighbourhood, each drifting away to our doors as we reached them. I was last. My parents were already asleep and I went to my room and sat on the bed with the flashlight in my hands.

Eventually, I nodded off with it on my lap, but not for long because there came a pounding on the front door. Outside the window, I could see Josh's dad's car. My dad came into my room a moment later.

"Josh's dad is downstairs. Were you with Josh earlier?"

I came clean immediately about everything except the wine. We went down and my dad summarised that evening's events. Josh's dad listened without comment or reaction.

He worked on Tour Hill as a custodian and was the same age as my dad. But he looked much older. He smoked a rolled cigarette and rubbed the back of his hand across his forehead. Losing a child is a horror that can't be explained in words. To also be accused, without evidence, of being the cause of that loss, would break any parent.

"Can you show me where you went in?" he asked quietly, almost like he was shy. "I want to go look... It's a big school, and in the dark... It's a big school." He risked a glance at my dad, who had his arms crossed.

"I'll get my coat," my dad said reluctantly. He had work in a few hours too and needed sleep. I felt responsible for Josh and terrible that I could be culpable in his disappearance. If I hadn't run, or gone with him, this poor man wouldn't be worried about losing yet another son.

"I'll go dad. You stay. I'll go," I said.

He paused and hesitated and looked at the weary father. How could he refuse? My father never talked about what he thought had happened to Mark. Neither did he declare this man's innocence. I could see him wrestling with the decision.

"Dad, it's fine," I told him. "We'll be right back." If he insisted on coming, it would only show what he really thought of the man begging for help.

"Okay," he said finally.

I got my coat and followed Josh's dad to the blue Chevy on the street. The gray leather seats were shiny, and the interior smelled like petrichor mixed with soap and cigarettes. A pile of butts filled the ashtray; it was the only unkempt spot I could see.

"Mind if I smoke?" He asked and lit up before I could say if I did or not, so I didn't answer. We drove the few blocks to Lakeside in silence and I pointed out where we'd gone. We got out of the car. Our footfalls crunched gravel and hissed through slick grass gone wild. When we came to the window, he stared at it and puffed away.

"Why'd you go in there?" he asked as he exhaled another plume.

"I don't know," I lied. I didn't want to tell him it'd been Josh's idea. "We were bored, I guess."

He shook his head like he didn't believe me. "He talk about the basement door again?"

He knew. "Yes," I admitted.

"He wanted to go in there, and see?"

"Yeah."

He crushed the unfinished butt under his heel, and seemed to choose his next words carefully. "Thing is... I think he's right."

"Oh?"

"Yeah, it's the only way... that day makes any sense. I bet he found something. Maybe that's why he hasn't come out yet. Maybe he took it to the police already."

"Um, did the police ever look down there?"

He shook his head. "They said they did but I heard something different. Nobody seriously looked for Mark. In their minds, they already knew who did it." A subtle smile appeared on his face, barely visible in the moonlight.

"Sir," I said, uncertain.

"Call me Joel," he said.

That didn't feel right, calling an adult by their first name, so I just went on with the question. "Why do people think you had something to do with Mark's disappearance?"

Exhaustion and the awkwardness of the moment were behind my asking. I don't think I would have talked at all otherwise. But we were standing around when we should have been searching for Josh.

"A dumb mistake on my part," he said. "The day Mark went missing, I went into work and began my shift like usual. Only, I wasn't supposed to be there. It was a Tuesday. I don't work Tuesdays. Not unless it's the busy season. I went in and when people figured Mark's gone, no one could find me because I'm busy cleaning the haunted house and it's dark in there even with the lights on. It's tough to clean the haunted house. Takes a long time. I get home a little late and find out about Mark and how everyone's been looking for me. Nobody believes I went to work by mistake. Nobody can recall seeing me that day on Tour Hill."

Joel clucked his tongue as if he couldn't believe his bad luck. "One little mistake. I only kept my job because my boss is old and not too with it, if you know what I mean. He calls me Joe most of the time." His hands dug in the front pocket of his shirt for a silver cigarette case.

Before he could light it, I got bold. "We should go and find Josh." I indicated the broken window.

Joel coughed and his reply came when he was ready. "I'll get a light from my trunk." He walked off and flicked open his lighter as he went. A moment later he returned with a flashlight, a tool bag, and a lit cigarette.

When I eyed the bag, slung over his shoulder, he explained. "You said the basement door was locked, and Josh broke it down. What if there are other locks?"

That made sense, but sense and truth are two different animals. I couldn't blame bad wine for my growing unease. Nevertheless, we climbed through the window and the vandalized mannequin heads were there to greet us.

In no time, we found the busted down door with the warning to keep it shut. Joel didn't seem to be in any hurry, and I found myself going first even though I didn't have the flashlight.

Fog from my breath expressed the low temperature. It smelled earthy too, like we were outside. The end of the flashlight beam gradually exposed a small shabby room with a heavy door on the right and an open passage in front.

"Josh!" I called.

"Shh!" Joel hissed in my ear. He was too close and his nicotine cloud clotted my nostrils.

"What?" I asked, sounding more irritated than was respectful.

"We don't know who else might be down here," he said seriously.

That made sense too. It was the same worry I had before.

We walked into the open doorway and found a long room full of broken desks and old furniture and something that looked like an exposed dumbwaiter on the far wall. Joel encouraged me to look into the rectangular opening with him and his hand rested against the small of my back. I looked at him, trying to communicate my discomfort, but his eyes were fixed on the shaft below.

"I don't see anything," I said.

He found a broom handle and poked down, finding the shaft filled in with dirt and garbage. "He didn't go down here."

Back in the other room, we turned our attention to the heavy, red door. It had an external locking mechanism, a bar that lifted when the handle latch was pressed. Josh could have easily walked inside and been immediately locked in.

The sense of a conclusion at hand faded, however, when I opened the door. A low ceilinged passage, a ramp that curved gently to the right, revealed itself to the flashlight, and Josh wasn't there. I heeded Joel's warning and didn't call out again, though I wanted to.

A heavy click came from behind next, and pure dread mixed with my disbelief. I rounded on Joel, who wore a mask of shadow behind the light he commanded. He'd let the door lock us in.

"Oops," he said. No regret could I detect in his tone. "Good thing I brought my tools."

I didn't agree. I couldn't speak. Something was very wrong here. "Josh!" I yelled. "Josh!"

"Hey, what did I say before?" Joel grabbed my bicep and squeezed and it hurt.

"Josh!" I continued, pulling away.

"You little-"

I took off up the ramp, walking swiftly, afraid that running might serve as an accusation, a trigger. After bumping my head off a low hanging pipe, I sensed the room opening up into a larger space. A draft invited me to the left, and I followed, tripping over some other utility feature of the school basement, and crashing my shoulder painfully into what may have been the quiet and cold furnace.

The beam of the flashlight appeared at the mouth of the hallway ramp, and I crawled away, following my nose toward cool air. Eventually, the surface beneath my hands changed from painted concrete to soil. There was a light up ahead, and an exit.

"Come back," Joel shouted as if I was being ridiculous. His light had found me and filled the old utility tunnel I'd crawled into. The pipes and electrical looked to have already been removed; they were valuable, so the school board took them first. I didn't listen but he was upright and fast. I'd only made it to the mouth of the exit when he seized the back of my collar and hauled me onto my feet.

He turned me around to look at him. Joel's lungs pulled in too much air, and he coughed. He placed the flashlight between his knees, and the beam lit up his face and wobbled while he extricated a cigarette from the silver case.

"I know what you're thinking, boy," he said. The pupils in his eyes were so expanded it was like looking at a shark. He lit up the cigarette, and then put a hand inside his tool bag. The muscles in his forearms twisted and stood out; his hand gripped something firmly in there.

Before I could see what, however, I heard, of all things, my dad calling me from afar. I'd forgotten about the other light I had seen when crawling in the tunnel.

Joel's demeanor changed swiftly. "Hey! We're over here!"

My dad didn't respond to the obvious. "I found Josh! He's here! He's not hurt." Joel and I walked together, and, sure enough, Josh sat on the ground beside my dad's legs. Never have I ever been so grateful for my dad's existence. I put him between Joel and myself immediately.

Joel knelt down by his son, and seemed to check him out. "You okay, boy?"

"Dad?" I asked and he understood the question.

After Joel and I had left, my dad couldn't sleep, so he reconsidered his decision to let me go alone. He didn't know where to look though and eventually heard Josh crying in the woods, near the exposed opening of the utility tunnel. Josh didn't seem physically hurt.

"I can't get him to talk, Joel," my dad said. "I think he got really scared."

Joel nodded and exhaled smoke, almost into his kid's face. "The door locks behind you in there. It's pretty dark without a flashlight."

Josh began to whisper softly and kept shooting me furtively glances from behind his pulled up knees. Joel stood up with the clear intention of finishing his cigarette.

I crouched beside Josh and rested a hand on his shoulder. "You alright, Josh?"

"Nothing, nothing, nothing," he kept saying over and over.

"Josh, what are you-"

His dad was suddenly done with his cigarette and pulling Josh to his feet. Arm wrapped around his son, Joel escorted Josh back to the school and the parking lot. My dad and I followed and went to our own car. There were no farewells or see you tomorrow.

We all went home and I didn't see Josh the same as he'd been again. He didn't get back to school, and only occasionally appeared outside his house, often at night, wandering back to Lakeside. His family became the target of gossip with renewed vigour and Joel's fears about his job were realised when his boss died and the new boss fired him the very next day. He turned to drinking more and he, of course, kept up with the cigarettes. He died before reaching sixty and the house was sold.

Life resumed for everyone else. Fred and Rex and I continued school, graduated, went to college, got jobs, got married, got divorced (in Rex's case), had children, and watched our own parents get old and pass away. Then we were suddenly old too and our children had children, and we found ourselves almost back where we'd started in Bridal Veil Lake: Friends with too much time on their hands.

What we decided to do, one random autumn day, was go for a walk in the woods. What actually happened is we walked directly to what was left of Lakeside Middle School.

The building had been demolished down to its foundation. Currently, all that can be easily found is a corner with a few faucets sticking out of the stone. Trees and grasses have consumed everything else. My grandchildren pretend not to believe me when I tell them I used to go to school there and say I'm so old I went to school in the woods.

We saw a man standing on the path, staring at the foundation corner. It was like he was waiting. Like he somehow knew we would come. Or maybe he'd been coming every day since '63.

He was as old as us, and we knew him instantly. Afraid he could disappear if disturbed, we approached cautiously, and didn't say a word.

When we were standing side by side again, he finally spoke.

"There was nothing down there," he said. "Nothing at all."

"I know, Josh. I know."

• • • •

EDITOR'S NOTE:

• • • •

STATISTICIANS SUGGEST a number of serial killers are never caught; their killing only ends because of poor health and death.

On the other hand, innocent people are accused and convicted of murder all the time.

The Perfect Student Doesn't Exist

I THOUGHT IT WAS A prank, so I played along at first.

"I don't bite," I told them. "You can sit here." I pointed to the empty desk dead center and at the front of the class, directly in front of my desk.

They - my first class as a certified teacher - all stared.

"Miss," said Beth, a big girl, shy and anxious, "Roy is sitting there."

I chuckled. They looked confused. Sweat gathered in the small of my back.

"Okay, then." I began the lesson. When it came time to hand out a worksheet, Beth raised her hand again.

"Miss, you forgot Roy." She deflated in response to my darkened expression.

I dropped the remaining pile of assignments on my desk. It wasn't as loud as I thought it would be. "I've already lost patience with this game. Beth, see me after class."

Work began, and many glanced toward the empty desk with worried faces. Progress was very slow. A few had put down their pencils. This work was easy. I didn't understand.

"What is the problem, folks?"

I looked to Beth, but I'd effectively destroyed that relationship before it began.

Another girl, Savannah, more confident, rebellious even, jutted out her chin before she spoke. "How can you just ignore someone?"

"What?"

She pointed at the empty desk. "He's been sitting there and, like, just looking sad this whole time, and you're okay with that? Seriously." Defiant, she waited for my response.

"As I stated earlier," I said, calmly, firmly, "I've had enough shenanigans." Before Savannah could speak, I pointed toward the exit. "Get out. Principal's office. Now."

The girl swore under her breath as she collected her things and left. I paged the office and told them the girl was on her way for disrespect. None of the other kids would meet my eye.

I sat at my desk and waved my hand at them dismissively. "Finish your work." This was going to be a difficult class. It was my first, however, so maybe that was to be expected.

As I gradually rallied my spirits and gathered my composure, the vice-principal appeared in the classroom doorway, beckoning me toward the hallway with his finger. He didn't look happy.

When I stepped out, Savannah was there, arms crossed; she'd been crying.

"Savannah says you're intentionally ignoring a student in your class," the VP stated.

I shook my head. "Sure," I said, trying to keep the situation light, "I'll show you." I backed into the classroom and pointed to the empty desk. "There he is."

The VP's eyes narrowed as he took in the sight. "Go back to your desk, Savannah." I was invited into the hallway for a more private chat. "I know you're new," he said, "and maybe this is some modern technique out of teacher's college I don't know about yet, but at Buchner Collegiate we address all students, and make everyone feel like they're worth our time and consideration."

I was confused and thought he hadn't understood. "Of course. I would never -"

"Good," he said. Like so many principals, he ended the conversation abruptly and walked off, some kind of short man's flex over someone perceived as lesser. It was only my first day, but I decided I did not like this VP.

Frustrated, I returned to class and dropped an assignment on Roy's desk."

"There ya go, Roy," I said, emphasizing the last word. The period ended, and the next group came in. Once again, the desk at the front remained empty. I didn't say anything and went ahead with the lesson.

A hand went up slowly after I handed out another assignment.

"Yes?"

"You missed someone," the boy said.

I sighed. "Let me guess. Roy?" I gestured with the pile of papers to the empty desk. The kid looked to his colleagues for support before reluctantly nodding. Again, I dropped a worksheet on the empty desk, on top of the first one from the previous period. "There we go. All better?" I didn't wait for an answer before moving on.

The next class, after lunch, and the desk remained vacant. I beat them to the punchline and made sure "Roy" got a copy of the assignment, and nobody objected. At last, I thought the ordeal had ended.

Then I was paged to the office. The VP and the principal were waiting at a round table. They wanted to discuss my student.

"Roy Vine," the VP said. "Students have been coming all day to say you've been mistreating him, neglecting him."

"What? That's ridiculous."

The principal lifted her finger. "All students need our attention, compassion, and understanding." She folded her hands and glanced around like a disappointed parent.

I was the kid in this scenario. "Roy doesn't exist," I told them. "It's some kind of prank. There's just an empty desk where he supposedly sits. And I didn't neglect him. I put assignments out for him all day, just to try and end the joke. I'll show you."

Reluctantly, they agreed to go with me to my classroom. The assignments were still there with one major difference: All of them were completed. All of them were signed by Roy.

My classroom had been locked. No one had been in or out. I begged them to let me see the footage, and it only confirmed this fact.

The most damaging information against me and my sanity, however, came in the form of a file containing Roy's personal information.

On paper, he exists. There's no photo and no birth date provided, but there is a phone number.

I called it after my disastrous meeting and admonishment with the admin. There's only static on the other end, static and a distant voice I strain to hear, speaking words of evil, detailed descriptions of horrific mutilation on people and animals, read like a grocery list.

Sometimes, it's just names. Names of students who would later die in the same car crash. One went missing.

It's all very tragic, I'm assured by colleagues and admin, but nothing more.

Pretty sure I lost my mind after that. Kept my job though. Fun fact: You can still be a teacher without sanity. It might even be encouraged.

No one questions why a student would be in all three of my classes, over and over. I've been a teacher for fifteen years as I write this email. Roy's been there every time. I know because everyone else can apparently see him, or, at least, knows he's there.

I even tried getting rid of his desk, but room is always made or a custodian brings an extra. Roy will sit in the back but prefers the front.

He does his work when I'm not there and earns strong results. In fact, he's my top student and always passes with ease. Yet he'll never graduate and never go away.

What should I do?

I Only See Roy

I RECENTLY SAW YOUR post on behalf of a teacher, concerning a student at Buchner Collegiate. His name is Roy Vine.

The account concerns me deeply because I believe it comes from a new custodian at the school, posing as a teacher.

I am the head custodian and only got the job last summer myself. In fact, a lot of the staff is new, including the principals and some of the teaching staff.

Apparently, there was an incident last year, around this time in fact, involving missing students and the previous vice principal. There isn't much more than gossip, however, as a judge instituted a media ban concerning whatever happened.

Must have been really bad though. Half the staff is gone, retired, quit, or transfered.

Those that remain don't talk about it.

But I digress.

This is about Charlotte. And Roy.

She's in her early twenties and never graduated high school. I didn't hold that against her. Neither did the new principal. Charlotte is quiet, polite, and completes her work without complaint.

That's what's so surprising about her standing at the head of a darkened classroom, on our night shift, teaching grammar to no one. Or, almost no one.

I watched her through the wire laced window at the side of the door. She looked as anxious as usual, angry even. I couldn't make out what she was saying as she strode around the room, handing out sheets of blank paper.

It was kind of cute, at first. Charlotte was living out some fantasy; she wanted to be a teacher. Cool.

But then she returned to the head of the class and dropped a pile of papers on the student desk at the front.

"Enough!" Charlotte shrieked. It was loud enough to make me flinch. "There's nobody there!"

I didn't move. She looked sweaty, and angry enough to make me afraid to be noticed.

That's when I realized Charlotte wasn't alone. A shadow so dark and small sat in the desk I thought was empty.

Its head turned, revealing red cinder eyes suggesting an undersized child's head. Any thought of this being a real kid vanished within the void that split its face, a grin that would agonize any real person, so dark the interior drank the light cast by its eyes.

I'm not ashamed to let you know, I walked away, and fast. It's not like horror movies. My brain checked out, and I went right back to sweeping the floor along the hallways. The shock of the experience didn't hit me until I tried to sleep, and found that thing behind my eyelids, smiling at the despair it caused.

I didn't sleep then, and had trouble for weeks after. These troubles, however, paled in comparison to what was coming.

Charlotte didn't seem overly bothered. She remained quiet and solitary. The only odd thing I noticed on dayshift was her worrying over papers, marking them up, and muttering under her breath. She was subtle about it; I think I'm the only one who noticed because I saw her "teaching."

The night shift cleanings afterward, I glimpsed in the same classroom and saw her but didn't stop to look in. Once was enough.

I did find a phone number on one of the pages she left in our breakroom. At the time, I hadn't seen the email Charlotte had written to you, Mr. Cleriot. I didn't know.

Charlotte's behaviour obviously bothered me. When I saw the number, I thought I could call it and get a clue about the kind of person she was or, I admit, find something that might result in her firing. No Charlotte, no Roy, right? I know now what I didn't know then.

I dialed.

A torrent of static and interference answered, as described in the previous email. There was a voice beneath it all too, a woman's I think. She only said one thing clearly, however: My name. Over and over, my name, first and last.

Charlotte wrote that misfortune befell those whose names were spoken.

She was right. Misfortune came. And won't go away.

In between my phone call and seeing her post and emailing you, I have become completely afraid of everything in Buchner Collegiate.

It started with a simple "accident" or something one would normally attribute to an accident: My mop snapped in half just as I averted my gaze from the classroom in question and Charlotte within.

I'd been pressing down on the mop, obviously, and, when it gave, I fell over, impaling myself in the gut. The wound was far from fatal but there was blood and the broken shaft was stuck into my body, so I screamed.

Charlotte arrived and started first aid. She didn't list that as one of her skills. Her voice was more confident than usual too and soothing. Like a teacher's.

I saw Roy, that thing, lurking behind her. I writhed to get away but she wouldn't let me. The charred hand of the shadow boy reached and touched the top of my foot.

I think I passed out.

The paramedics were suddenly there, and, somehow, Charlotte and Roy were not. I was taken to the hospital to have the handle removed. That's where I discovered an odd discolouration on my foot, a burn the size of a dime or fingertip.

I was off work for a few days but had to return, sadly limping around and in pain. I needed the money. The principal called me to the office that day. Charlotte was there. She wouldn't look at me. I stood in the doorway, frozen, even after being invited to sit down.

"Still feeling rough," he said. "That's why I called you here. Charlotte filled in while you were in hospital, and, well, we know you need to work, so the solution is for Charlotte to take over as temporary head custodian while you recover. Your salary will be the same, of course, but you'll be on light duty, and won't have to deal with scheduling and supplies. How does that sound?"

I hadn't stopped looking at Charlotte and would have agreed to anything to get away from her.

I should have told them to stuff it because suddenly I was scheduled to work every night shift. Normally, all the custodians took such a week in pairs once a month.

Now it's all me and Charlotte and Roy.

Charlotte continues to "teach" every night. As soon as she locks up Buchner, she goes to the classroom, leaving me to do everything. I don't dare complain, even as every shadow in the halls seems to whisper and move and watch.

The brooms feel brittle. The burn doesn't heal. Roy - whatever it is - occupies my thoughts and doesn't let me sleep.

I can't quit. Yes, I need the money, but I'm more afraid of pissing it off again. I think it wants me to stay, but won't hesitate to harm me if I try to disrupt its time with Charlotte.

It caused the mop to break. I know that. But it expected me to bear the wound silently. The whispers tell me so.

I am taking a huge risk in contacting you, Cleriot.

I need help.

Any suggestions would be appreciated.

This can't go on forever.

The Hanging

WE FOUND PAL IN THE morning, hanging by his leash over the top of his kennel fence. Pal was a big mutt and scared us when he got out because he ran around like wild. My friend's dad didn't take Pal out of the kennel much, so the dog had been escaping often.

There'd been some complaints from neighbours, so it looks like Pal's owner had come up with a leash as the solution. Too bad he didn't tell Pal about it. The dog must have hopped the fence as per usual and hung himself. Or so we all thought.

Pal's death became the focus of conversation on Ferry Street. Feelings were mixed about his passing. He had bitten a few kids, nipped at their fingers, eager to play with someone.

I used to think my friend would have taken care of Pal fine, if he'd been allowed to. But his dad was a tool, rarely home, and often drunk when he was.

A week later, a pet tragedy struck my household. Our black cat, Zoomie, was run over in the street. My mom buried him in the gorge, she said, though I doubt she really took her that far.

It wasn't the best summer for animals on our street. Less than five days later, a dog got hit by a car. It didn't die right away but had to be put down later. The owner lived four houses away and didn't understand how his dog had gotten out of the yard. It was a little dog and quite content on a shady deck with a fan while his owner was at work. It'd never tried to leave before.

When another cat was hit the following week by a car and killed, people started to get kind of freaked and kept closer eyes on their pets.

Honestly, I didn't think too much about it. I liked Zoomie, of course, and missed her but was more preoccupied with my friends and playing outside. My friend, Sean, sort of disappeared after his dog died; we didn't think much of it because he had a Nintendo and thought he was just playing it all the time.

47

One afternoon, however, it was too hot to play street hockey anymore. The game broke up early, and I went into our backyard to drench myself with the hose.

Sean was there, talking to my youngest brother, who was only six, half our age. I got an instant bad feeling. They didn't see me yet, so I stuck close to the big pine tree and crept closer to listen.

"Say 'shit,'" Sean instructed my little brother.

"Shit," my brother said.

I lost it. I leaped out of hiding and clocked Sean in the back of the head. He fell and smacked his forehead on one of the big limestone rocks we had in our yard for no reason. He calmly stood up while blood poured over his right eye and started walking away.

"Walk faster," I said.

I asked my brother what had happened, but he was frightened by what he didn't understand. I took him inside and told my mom about it. She went next door and bitched out Sean's dad but he was drunk and didn't understand, so, no discipline for Sean came after.

"Keep a closer eye on your brother," my mom said.

"Sure. He can come to hockey."

My mom gave me a look but didn't say anything.

The next day, my little brother came to hockey out front of our house. He was disappointed when he didn't get to play and didn't want to be the referee or the commentator. I promised to buy him a popsicle if he waited till the first game was over.

He was gone within ten minutes and I didn't notice. One of my friends pointed out his absence. I didn't run to my house. I went to Sean's. His stupid dad answered the door and thought I wanted Sean. He kept calling him and calling him and disappeared inside to look for his son.

I ran around the side of the house to the backyard and found Sean there with my little brother. He was in the kennel on top of the dog house with the leash around his neck and the other end tied to a steel ring.

"Come on, climb up, you can do it," Sean said to him from outside the kennel. So this was how Pal had died and the other pets too. Sean has coaxed them to their deaths and when people got suspicious he escalated to new prey.

If we found my little brother hanging like Pal, there'd be a great deal of scrutiny but also a pretty good chance it'd be written off as an accident, a little kid imitating what he'd seen. He didn't understand that Pal had been dead when we found him that morning.

My brother reached up the chain link fence and grabbed a hold of the top bar.

"Good job," Sean said, "you're so strong. Keep going." The bastard smiled.

Those were the last words I ever heard from Sean because I beat him so severely. I think I would have killed him if my mom hadn't stopped me.

My little brother still had the leash around his neck and hadn't gotten down from the doghouse. He cried and cried.

Lucky for me, my mom understood what had been about to go down and who was responsible. Sean was unconscious and bloody when his dad came out. He saw the leash too. He wasn't so drunk that he didn't get it either.

"I'm sorry," was all he said before collecting his son, tossing him into the car, and driving off. We never saw him or Sean in the neighbourhood again. The house went up for sale and movers collected the crap inside. A new family moved in and they were nice.

The only reason I know Sean didn't die from my attack that day is because I ran into him a few years later at a bar on Tour Hill. He recognized me and smiled before patting something on the bar. I thought he was inviting me over to sit. Little did he know I wasn't too old to give him another beating.

He left fast, however, using a backdoor patio entrance and hopping the fence to escape. He'd forgotten two things on the bar. Or maybe left them for me to find: A whistle and stop sign paddle.

The psycho had become a crossing guard.

Now I recognize this isn't really weird in the supernatural sense, but I thought it was crazy enough for you to look into since your ad said you and your friends are investigating all the weird stuff that's happened in Bridal Veil Lake

Plus, Sean is still out there, and I think we both know nobody seems really interested in putting away the psychos in this town.

I have two school age daughters, Mr.Cleriot. They both walk to school, and there are three crossing guards they meet along the way.

None of them are Sean. But what if one suddenly is on some random day? People get sick. Crossing guards probably fill in for ill coworkers all the time.

I tried calling the city but they won't give me any info, even after I told them my story.

I can't quit my job. I'm a single dad. I can't be with them every second of the day.

He left his paddle and whistle at the bar, though. What the hell does that mean?

How else might he lure my kids, or yours, to their deaths?

Grandma Found A Faerie Fort

WE TOOK MY GRANDMA to the western part of the gorge forests because it's quiet. If you know anything about Bridal Veil Lake, you'll know there are places for tourists and the spots residents try to keep for themselves.

My grandmother has or had bad dementia. She used to love to play in the woods as a girl. We thought it'd be a good thing to bring her for the afternoon, and it was going well. Even before we left, she picked out a fresh tracksuit and put on all her jewelry, including multiple rings on the same fingers.

Most days she spent watching TV and never saying a word. That morning she sang. I wasn't about to tell her how weird she looked with all her old world bling.

She perked up more when I pulled into the lot. "Cindy, we're here!" she said to my mom, her daughter. Cindy, one of her best friends from childhood, died twenty years ago. My mom's name is not Cindy.

Before we could unpack the trunk for a St.Patrick's Day picnic by the river, Grandma took off. She's eighty-eight and frail. To see her jog into the trees defied reasoning, and was kind of hilarious, at first.

Figuring she couldn't get far - I've seen her fail to negotiate the step up from the sunken living room - we resumed packing up and then followed her.

The gorge forest is split down the middle from west to east by the Black River, which empties out into the basin lake, where the town's namesake comes from: A bridal veil waterfall.

I worried a little about Grandma falling in and being swept away. The mild winter hadn't brought the spring floods but the river took lives every year. This spring, I had no doubt, would be no different.

Beneath the shade of the canopy, we could see Grandma had already disappeared.

"Oh god," my mom said as she clutched her fists against her cheeks and looked toward the river. It was still far off though. No way she made it all that way over the short hills and roots and rocks. More than likely, she was sprawled in one of the lows or resting against a tree.

"Grandma!"

"Mom!"

So the search began. We walked right to the loose gravel shore and found no trace of her. My mom started to panic and so did I, which led to a bad choice. I went west. She went east. The direction I chose got more wild, and harder to traverse. It didn't occur to me that Grandma probably wouldn't plough through thickets and dead branches.

I was more worried about my mom. East along the river would eventually bring her to the paths beneath the overpasses. Below those bridges were these weird alcoves some genius designed without criminals in mind.

Joggers and hikers had been ambushed there and mugged. It was pretty far. I kept telling myself I'd turn around after the next tree, the next hill, etcetera.

My oblivious ignorance of the difficulty moving forward turned out to be fortunate, or so I thought. It would have been better if I never found my grandmother.

I pushed through a clutch of purple creeper thorns (don't know their proper name), and found a muddy deer track with human footprints and a familiar pair of teal slip-ons.

"Grandma!" I called.

I heard a giggle that turned out to be her. At the mouth of a creek feeding the river, my grandmother crouched on a wide, flat slab of limestone.

Her face covered in red, she held a tiny, struggling thing, which ceased to resist when her bony hands ripped it in half.

"Grandma!" I figured she'd managed to snag a small animal. "Stop!"

She did, long enough for me to get closer and see the tiny limbs twitching. They were human but impossibly small. Fingers and fingernails no bigger than a dime were amidst the gore. Grandma pinched the pieces like horderves and popped them into her mouth.

I think I said something like, "What the hell?"

Grandma grinned, and her teeth were all red. "Try some, Aaron." She dug into her track pants pocket and pulled out a very tiny person. I felt my skin prickle with a chill despite the warmth of the breeze.

I don't know how to write this next part in a way that's believable. It was a tiny woman, smaller than my hand, a Tinkerbell without wings (because Grandma had already torn them off). Caught in the old woman's fist, she chirped like a mouse as her head was severed by dentures.

"Oh, it's good, it's good," Grandma remarked as she swallowed and drank from the stump as if it were one of those liquor bottles found in hotel room fridges.

All around her on the stone were the body parts of the little people. Blood ran over the side of a hollow tree. Clouds raced across the sky and blotted the sun. Whatever fucked up thing had just happened, it was time to go.

Beyond panic, I entered a yet unexperienced level of shock. I didn't notice how bad my hands were shaking until I tried to use them to brush the limbs from her hair. I should have left them for evidence, so I could explain what really happened that St.Patrick's Day.

Instead, when I caught up with my mom, she quite reasonably lost her shit and figured what I had: A delusional lady caught a rat or something and thought it was dinner. I didn't even try to explain. I stayed quiet and let her escort Grandma to the car and drive us all to the hospital.

The nurse on duty saw the excessive blood and got us to the doc fast. I've never not had to wait in the ER before. Another nurse assessed while cleaning, discovering quickly no injuries on Grandma. Questions followed, obviously. Where had so much blood come from?

I had to answer, and I lied. How could I tell them what really happened?

"A raccoon, I think."

Combined with her advanced dementia, the nurse seemed to accept the explanation, and ordered a bunch of needles to ensure Grandma didn't get rabies amongst other infections. That's when her clarity returned, I'm sure of it. She didn't want the shots and objected.

"I don't need them," she said to the nurse, who only smiled patiently before explaining that she did because of what she'd possibly eaten or been exposed to. "Those little shits? I've done it before. How do you think I've lived so long? Not from exercise or avoiding vices, I tell you." Her laughter sounded crazier than ever. They forced her to get the shots. We went home.

It started that very night. I couldn't find anything. My toothbrush, pajamas, the remote, some melatonin pills, and all the accessories of my routine had been moved around. For my mom, it was the same.

"It's like we were robbed," she said, "but nothing was taken. Only hidden." There wasn't much time to think about it because Grandma went straight to the vodka in the freezer and started pouring shots.

"Mom! Stop! You can't mix thatvwith your meds!"

Grandma chuckled and raced around the kitchen island with her shot and didn't spill a drop, except down her gullet. "That burns so good."

"Mom!"

They argued some more. Grandma winked at me and went to bed. Mom poured us some shots, though I'm not of age to drink, and we sat quietly before going upstairs too. I couldn't sleep. The wifi was out and my data was slow. The King novel I'd been reading wasn't where I left it, but I was too tired to search.

The tiny bodies had been ripped to shreds. She drank their blood. It couldn't have happened. Another surge in panic kept the air trapped behind my firmly clenched teeth. I marched downstairs, intending to hit the bottle.

But Grandma had beat me to it.

"Hey," she said, lounging in her recliner with the vodka on her knee. None of the lights were on, and I jumped when she spoke.

I wanted to call her out for taking off earlier, and all the headache that followed. My mother and I, however, had become accustomed to not speaking to her about anything seriously. The tone we often took was similar to when one speaks to a dog. We didn't think she understood.

And that was wrong. It partially explains her resentment toward us and what followed next.

She glided to the front door and flicked on the living room lights. A stranger put on my grandmother's coat. The woman looked like my mom but younger. She still had on the rings and necklaces from earlier in the day, coagulated blood and all.

"More will be coming. You should go. They'll take revenge on loved ones. They don't remember me or what a bad bitch I am. See, I don't love anyone more than myself. Sorry." She shrugged as if relaying an immutable fact of life. "Bye kid." The vodka went too.

That was the last time I saw her, whatever she was or had become. Mom was hysterical in the morning and pretty pissed off that I could be so detached. She became more angry when she couldn't find her phone or her keys. We don't have a landline, so she couldn't call the police.

My phone was also missing.

"What the hell is happening?" she asked me, and I told her to sit down. She did and that's when the power went out. "Great." A heavy knocking came from upstairs. It sounded like the table in the hallway had fallen over. The kitchen window began to splinter, glass grinding under an invisible pressure. We stared at it and then at one another.

"Oh god, they're coming," I said without really knowing who I meant. Mom gave little shakes of her head as something else fragile turned over and smashed in the living room.

Complete darkness washed over the window like a plague. If I hadn't seen them before, I might have thought they were locusts. They could have stayed invisible. They wanted us to see. A bit of glass plinked into the sink below as the first put its head inside.

Mom started to scream and I along with her. She raced to the utensils drawer and got out a knife. I saw our phones in there and scooped them up, thinking we could call for help.

The one that poked its head in flew like a dart at my mom's face, piercing her cheek with a black thorn. She snatched it off and threw it against the wall. The tiny body fell onto our steel serving tray, the one we always brought Grandma's food and meds on.

That's where it started to scream as the flesh melted off its tiny skeleton, steam rising from the boiling blood leftover.

Outside, the creatures' shrieks of fury sounded the same as a flock of angry birds. They pulled back for a final assault against the window.

Mom grabbed the serving tray and held it over the bleeding glass. "Forks! Spoons! Knives!" she yelled as her body braced the impromptu shield.

I ripped the drawers out of the cabinet, scattering half the utensils onto the floor. The big bottom drawer had our colanders and mixing bowls for pancakes and stomach flus.

"Mom!"

More creatures zipped in from the living room carrying sharpened sticks and stones.

Swinging the drawers did no real damage. I think the clatter of steel on steel made them hesitate.

"Run!" Mom yelled. Her whole arm was covered with them, gouging, tearing, scratching, biting. She screamed and intentionally fell onto the tray, crushing and searing the majority.

I pulled her up and we pushed through the clusters with frantic strikes, causing burns and leaving a trail of crushed bodies.

Our exit strategy changed swiftly when the front door burst off its hinges. A huge, bearded man with thick arms and an oily scalp bellowed out a warcry, charging straight for us. Mom belted him with the tray, bending it over his head. The deep throated growl turned to a high pitched wail of pain. He was one of them.

They can be different things, apparently. A number of these other forms swarmed in after the big man had been dropped to the hardwood by my mom.

Some were more or less human. Others retained the cutesy Tinkerbell form even while raging to kill us. Many others had bodies too strange to really describe. Some were like mists and shadows. Another moved like a ray of light.

"Upstairs!" Mom pushed me before despair and terror allowed an acceptance of our deaths. We raced through the upstairs hallways and into the bathroom. She locked the door and put her back to it.

"Into the tub!"

"What?! The window. It's not that far down."

More were pouring into the house. It would only be a matter of seconds before they figured out where we were.

Even if we hit the ground without injury, they'd be on us fast. Death was coming. Grandma had fucked us over so bad.

Mom pushed me into the bathtub. I fell on my face and felt the contents of the utensils against my back before I could turn over. She placed the colander on my head like a helmet, and dropped the rest into my lap.

The door cracked in half after that.

"I love you," she said, turning and charging toward the bulge of those tiny fuckers, leaping over the remaining half of door, and leading them away.

She didn't get too far. I heard a thump and the furious chirping ceased, replaced by thousands of prickling noises. They butchered the recognition from her body while I shivered and pissed myself in the tub.

I called 911 but didn't say anything.

The big guy with the beard and now badly burned head came in alone and saw me hiding beneath the scant layer of steel. I was shaking so hard. I don't think I'll ever stop being afraid. He touched his forehead and thought better of going near me, I guess. He stared for a long time. I closed my eyes.

"Kid," a woman that turned out to be a cop said, shining a flashlight in my face. It'd gotten dark outside and the power hadn't been restored.

I won't tell you every detail of what came next because I bet anyone can guess. The truth did nothing but convince them I'd lost my sanity and horrifically murdered and mutilated my mother.

I went through a trial. You won't find any mention of it in the news. Under the Youth Criminal Justice Act, the judge issued a complete publication ban.

Bridal Veil Lake is visited by hundreds of thousands of people a year. Those that actually live here are few. Media coverage would supposedly make it impossible to reintegrate into my community. I didn't bother telling the justice it wouldn't be possible anywhere.

Once I found out the institution I was going to had several layers of old, thick steel around it, I vowed to never leave again. In fact, I haven't willingly left my barred cell in years. I don't have to go unless the experts agree I can take care of myself.

Of that, they will never be convinced because I never stop talking about the faeries my grandma ate and how their flesh and bones and blood made her young again.

More significantly, I will not say I killed my mom like the doctor wants me to. He asks what happens and I tell this story from the beginning. He doesn't mind. He earns by the hour.

I'm writing to you, years now since it happened because another St.Patrick's Day has come and gone and in the midst of my endless mourning, I got a letter from someone containing a gold ring.

Some don't like gold was written on a napkin stuffed inside the envelope.

"Grandma," I said out loud as I studied the ring.

"No," the guard that delivered the mail said. "It was a young woman that dropped it off. I remember because who drops mail off personally to a place like this?"

I didn't tell him who.

I just gave him the ring.

And threw away the message.

Lady In The Leaves

I PLAYED OUTSIDE ALONE.

That was the unwritten rule.

When I was a kid, both of my parents worked from home. They preferred silence and strongly encouraged me to go outside after school. Between the ages of six and ten, I spent a few hours each day in the backyard, which kind of sucked.

The space was large and had half a dozen mature trees, but there wasn't much to do. Plus, the furthest end of the yard was all mud and roots from dead trees on the other side of the chain link fence.

The property on the other side looked abandoned. A portion of the small house in the opposing backyard had crumbled. It may have been a heritage ruin. There are a number of such rotting locations in Bridal Veil Lake. It's like the town makes them historical landmarks to avoid having to deal with them.

I never found the front of the property on the other side of the block, where all the houses are somewhat modern looking and clearly not wreckages of stone. The "heritage site" must be enclosed by a newer neighborhood or sitting on somebody's property, and they didn't want to deal with it any more than the town did.

Whatever the case, I usually avoided going to the back of my yard because it was creepy and easy to trip on the roots and fall into the sucking mud. My stressed-out parents weren't happy if I came in filthy, which, of course, limited play options further.

I generally sat on the limestone rocks I'd gathered from the back of the yard and waited to be allowed in, often watching the abandoned property for lack of a better option. Staring at my own house had also irked my parents for some reason.

On a gray day in January, when more rain than snow had fallen, I sat thinking about my Christmas toys inside my bedroom. It was foggy, and I couldn't see the back half of the yard.

"Aric," a woman's voice said quietly but clearly.

"Hello?" I thought somebody was calling from the other side of the fence. I'd never seen anyone back there, but it was possible. How she would know my name I didn't know, but it's not a huge town. Be pretty funny if the property I believed abandoned belonged to a friend's parents.

"Hello?" I asked again. I got off my rock and took a few steps to try and see better. No one responded. I got a shiver and nearly fell over when my dad was suddenly standing behind me.

"Come inside, Aric," he said. "It's supper time." He sounded irritated. I found out why when I got to the table and my mom was there, wearing the same expression.

"What were you doing outside?" my father asked. He unfurled his napkin with a wrist snap.

"Outside? Nothing." I wanted to add "as usual" but knew I'd get in trouble for it. Punishments were always chores and I didn't want to waste more time not playing with my new toys.

"What was all the noise then?"

"What noise?"

"Somebody screaming bloody murder," my mom said.

I shrugged. "I didn't hear any screams." Also, they heard screaming and didn't come outside to see if I was okay? I was too young at the time to understand the full assholes my parents were.

"Enough," my dad said. "You're clearly lying. Eat. We will discuss the consequences afterward."

There was no point in arguing. I ate, and only had to do the dishes after. Light punishment for lying, unless they didn't really believe I had. I finished up, played with my toys, and got ready for bed.

I had trouble falling asleep. I had to go to bed too early so my parents could pull some more hours of work in peace. The quiet play in my room was too distracting, obviously.

Wide awake, I crept to the window. It was dark outside and still foggy. Hours of my days were spent looking at nothing, I lamented. School was pretty boring. Recesses were too brief. Having friends over was forbidden. I wasn't allowed to go anywhere. I started to cry.

"Shhhhhhhhhhhh," a woman soothed. I saw no one, and yet my eyes were drawn to the yard below, where a shadowy figure now stood in the fog. "Don't cry, Aric," she said, but like directly into my ear. I swear I felt a gentle breath against my skin.

I didn't respond. I backed away from the window, slowly, and crawled into bed, pulling the blanket over my head. Pressure from a hand fell against my leg and stroked it gently. I was scared. But not enough to dare violate the silence my parents required.

I'd rather die, I realized.

The ghostly hand continued until I, at last, gave in to imagining a caring adult was comforting me. I slept but not through the night. Only a few hours passed when a prolonged cry of abject horror filled our home.

My parents, not yet finished work for the night, burst into my room together. The covers were ripped from my hands, and they both began with many false accusations.

There were too many to recall, but they all amounted to something like, "You don't care about this family."

"I wasn't screaming," I said. "Please listen. It wasn't me."

"Not another peep!" my father shouted before they left and slammed the door. I felt hopeless. Their disbelief put us all at risk. Somebody had screamed inside our house. Were we really just going to ignore it? Why wouldn't they believe me?

I got dressed. Let them die, I thought. I was done. This would be my first attempt at running away. Naturally, I would need money to begin a new life. I had none, but understood people might pay me for services rendered. I would be a painter. I put a single plastic tube of paint and a small brush into my coat pocket and was ready to go.

It was easier to escape out the back door. The backyard looked darker and filled with even thicker fog. I only had to walk down the side steps and around the deck to get to the driveway gate.

"Aric," the woman said. "Aric, don't leave me. I'm cold." Her voice was a loud whisper between my ears. "Aric, come. Please. Come and get me out. Aric, I'm stuck in the roots. The mud, Aric. Aric, Aric, Aric, Aric. Please."

She sounded so desperate. I went into the fog and to the muddy portion of the yard, tripping immediately on the first root to catch my foot. I landed in a pile of leaves, not realizing I'd reached the chainlink fence faster than expected.

My fingers felt smooth skin in the dark. I recoiled and stood up. There was a face in the leaves. Her mouth opened and closed like a fish; she was gasping for air.

"Are you alright?"

It was a dumb question.

"I'll call the police."

"Help me," she shrieked. It wasn't some telepathy this time. It was her mouth, her lungs.

I lurched further into the leaf pile, cold mud mouths sucking my shoes off. I was up to my knees and could see her face more clearly. She was young and pretty and utterly afraid.

How was she stuck? How was I going to get her out? As I stood there trying to figure out what to do, she continued screaming and my parents appeared from the fog.

"She's stuck," I told them urgently.

They were confused and appeared at a loss for words.

My hands found her arms beneath the pile.

That's when her expression changed from fear to childish glee. Something - not hands - grabbed me back and started to pull. It is so much easier to pull someone down than up. I fell into the leaves, my face against hers. She smelled of vegetation and soil and coppery blood.

"I was older when I found out," she whispered in my ear.

I fought hard against the roots pulling me down with her. I'm not sure if it was me that was able to spin around or if she - whatever she was - simply allowed it.

My parents were there. Just watching with a mixture of excitement and fear. Little smiles curved their lips.

I reached for them. "Help me."

My mother moved closer to my dad. He wrapped an arm around her shoulders and said something I couldn't hear into her ear.

The roots, her hands, continued pulling down until the dull light of night faded. I held my breath, buried under the mud.

"A little longer. You must know," she said.

The urge to draw air began fast; you use more oxygen when you're afraid. One breath of dirt would be the end, wouldn't it?

"You want to know what they said," the woman said, the lady of the leaves. "I can tell you but I think you already know. Does that make your choice easier?"

What choice? I only thought about the question.

She answered similarly. "The choice to stay with me, someone who loves you, or to go back."

With someone who doesn't.

She didn't confirm or deny the idea.

I want to live.

"So be it," she said.

Suddenly, I was breathing cold air rapidly and struggling to stay conscious. I was vaguely aware of my parents but couldn't be sure of what they were doing. There was a car ride or an ambulance, and then I was in a hospital, where I recovered.

The doctor explained I'd fallen and bumped my head. I nearly drowned in the mud until my dad pulled me up. With my parents in the room, there was no point in denying this version of events.

I waited until we were in the car to challenge them. "You didn't help me," I said as my mom pulled out of the parking lot.

"What's that?" my dad said, looking at his phone.

"When she pulled me into the mud," I said, "You just watched. You didn't help."

My dad finally looked at me. "Huh? What are you saying?"

"She was in the leaves," I said.

My father looked alarmed. "Who was in the leaves, Aric?"

"I don't know, a woman. A young woman. She pulled me under the mud with the tree roots and -"

"I think we should go back to the hospital," he said to my mom.

"He's just confused," my mom said. "We've been working too much. Our stress is becoming his." She faced the road. "We need to do better. Why was he outside in the first place?"

"There's a question," he said. "Why did you go out last night, Aric?"

"I... after the screaming... I heard..."

"Why were you screaming, Aric?"

"Let him answer," my mom chided my dad.

"Sorry, sorry, Aric."

"I wasn't screaming," I said. My parents exchanged a quick glance, and I knew it was over. I was outnumbered by superior foes. They had their narrative, and, to be fair, it made more sense than mine. Therapy was on the horizon.

My parents took some time off from work. I didn't have to go to school, and I got to stay in and play with my toys. We watched movies and ordered a lot of takeout. I was starting to feel better and accept that I really had been stressed out and confused to the point of hallucinating.

The following week, however, my dad wanted to show me something in the backyard. I hadn't been out there since that horrible night.

"Come on," he said. "I found something you'll want to see." He walked in front of me as we went to the back of the yard, obscuring the view until we were on top of the spot. A filthy mannequin head sat on top of the pile beside a one-armed plastic torso and a pair of legs.

"I haven't found the rest yet," my dad said. "I was wondering about what you'd said in the car and found the face right away. Why would somebody bury this here? And when? Must have been a long time ago. It was all tangled in roots.

I know what I saw. I remember the feel of her smooth cheek against mine. The house beyond the chain link fence, with its rotted trees, held a single shadow in a tiny window before it moved out of sight.

"It's for the best," I said.

"What?"

"That's what you whispered to mom. It's for the best. The lady in the leaves pulled me under. I begged you for help. And you said, 'It's for the best.'"

My dad looked guilty. He looked at the mannequin pile, evidence he must have planted, and gestured weakly in his defense. "I... Aric, you were confused. I'm sorry you think we'd... do something like that."

"Who was she?" I pushed. "Who is buried here?"

"I don't know what you're talking about," he said and walked away, leaving me again. I crouched by the mannequin for a moment before movement in the yard caught my eye.

She stood, unobscured, between the dead trunks, and naked except for some leaves and dirt in her hair, on her body. Her smile was mischievous and sad, if that makes any sense. I think maybe that's just the way her face is and why someone killed her.

They didn't like the way she smiled.

When my mom called from the back of the house, the lady waved and walked behind a tree. I did not see her again, but never forgot her lesson. My parents were not trustworthy.

AP CLERIOT

The years that followed were difficult. I ignored the clumsy attempts my parents made to repair our relationship and stayed out of the house and around Bridal Veil Lake as much as possible.

Therapy and medication only brought more clarity to confirm my suspicions of their motives. I went to the library often to try and learn about the property behind our home but couldn't find anything.

That's where I found your flyer, AP Cleriot.

I started searching through my parents' stuff when they were at work and I was supposed to be in school. That's when I found the photo. That's when I found my lady in the leaves again.

I waited until my eighteenth birthday to place the photo on the dinner table. They'd just finished putting down the cake, singing happy birthday.

"Who is she?" I asked.

But they didn't answer.

"I'm leaving," I told them. "It's for the best."

I haven't been back since, and I'm no closer to figuring out the identity of the lady and what happened to her.

Are You Big and Scary?

I'M IN NEED OF SOMEONE big and scary tonight, so I can do something mildly unsafe. Nothing illegal. Message me if interested.

That was the post on /rbridalveillake, where I've lived for about six years.

I was interested. I needed money, and I am both big and scary. Telling you exactly how tall I am, my weight, and whether or not I can throw a punch seems like a good way to prove I'm a weak, pathetic loser.

I definitely am a loser.

But I'm also big and scary.

I'm going down to the industry park near the shitty part of the river. Abandoned for like 70 years. Weird stuff going down there. I'm a journalist kind of. I want to get a closer look. Afraid to go alone

might be safer going alone than with a stranger on the internet, I messaged back.

you want the job or not?

yeah

meet at the old casino.

Where's that?

jeese, new in town?

kind of

She - Helga - explained the old casino meant the small one, the first Canadian attempt at gambling like the Americans.

The industry park she mentioned was like a separate and forgotten part of Bridal Veil Lake's history. Cars and steel used to be made there before the town went full tourist trap. Miles of weeds cracked the tarmac and pulled at rusted shut factories and warehouses.

She picked me up in a shitbox van and we drove to the southern peninsula of Bridal Veil Lake. The roads weren't maintained and parts had crumbled completely into muddy holes framed by small, twisted trees reclaiming the land.

We pulled up to a busted section of chain link fence folded down on a small hill. The headlights revealed the passage of many feet in the sucking mud. We got out of the van.

Helga turned out to be pretty big and scary too. She's definitely the tallest woman I've ever met and certainly not shy of the weightroom. Her leather jacket couldn't hide the muscles underneath. A camera dangled from her shoulder.

"We're here for pictures?"

"Good thing I didn't ask for smart too," she said, grinning and extending her hand. "Thormund, right?"

"Uh, yeah."

"Is that your real name?"

I didn't reply.

"You're not that scary."

"You're scarier than expected," I said. "You look like you can take care of yourself. Why the need for a hired goon?"

Her smile vanished. "Because nobody can watch their own back." In a surprise move, she gave me the cash in an envelope upfront.

"Awfully trusting," I said, tucking the envelope into my jacket.

"I can take care of myself," she quipped. "Besides, we're past the point of mistrust. If you wanted to take the money and run, you could."

Or worse, I thought.

This was a dangerous idea for anyone. Inviting a stranger that was both big and theoretically scary would attract the biggest assholes on the internet, I imagine.

Helga gave me a heavy-duty flashlight and strapped on a headband with a light clipped to the front. We sprang up and down as we walked over the wrecked fence. The muddy ground held onto a few sneakers.

"Looks like we're not the only visitors," I said to Helga's back. Her makeshift headlamp blinded me when she turned around. I pulled a child size shoe from the half-frozen muck.

"Keep going. Come on," she urged.

"What the fuck goes on here?"

Helga sighed and I could only see the plume of frosted air spout from her lips. "It's a bad place, Thormund."

"Is that why you're here? You want to see bad stuff?"

"Something like that," she said. "If I can get some evidence, then they'll have to listen to me, and they'll have to do something."

"Who will have to listen?"

"Chatty for a hired goon," she said, walking to the rusted corner of a sheet metal building. "Let's go."

I followed and did my best to be as quiet as her. Where we'd entered was filled with similar low ceilinged structures stuffed with old tires and trash. Something had died nearby. I could smell it.

She moved deliberately; she knew where she was going. A garage once used for large vehicles loomed beyond a row of tightly packed dumpsters. We squeezed through one of the narrow passages. A door had been propped open with a broken cinder block.

Someone had put that there.

I began to feel uneasy. There were too many blindspots, places to ambush two idiots with flashlights.

Helga pointed to a service ladder bolted to the side of the garage. I shook my head. Her headlamp bobbed up and down as she nodded. Then she shut off her light and mounted the first rung.

Damn it. I turned off the chunky flashlight and tucked it behind the ladder. Screw climbing with one hand. I hadn't worn gloves. Cold rust flakes dug into my palms as I followed Helga to a sagging, tar paper roof.

"Don't walk in the center," she whispered, pointing to a small pond gravity had made on the roof.

I gave her a thumbs up she probably couldn't see.

She stuck close to the edge, practically using the steel flashing like a tightrope. I had more faith in the rotting surface than my balance and chose a middle ground between the rainwater pool and the possibly fatal drop off the side.

When we'd worked our way around to the back of the building, Helga sprawled out and peered into a hole. A dim light illuminated her sharp features. She snapped a few photos before gesturing for me to come and have a look.

I shook my head.

She jabbed her index finger against the tar paper. I felt like a dog being summoned. So why did I obey? I admit feeling instant attraction to Helga.

Are you starting to see how I'm a loser yet?

Yeah, I crawled beside her, not because I wanted to look in the hole, but for other, obvious reasons not appropriate to our circumstances.

And it only got worse.

It took a few moments to understand what we were looking at. A fire burned in a cinder block fire pit. Surrounding the flames were tightly packed ranks of children. Less than a dozen held out their hands to the flames for warmth. Hundreds more squatted and hugged their knees in the dark behind them.

As far as I could see, every square foot of the garage interior had a child in it. Their squeezed together bodies provided a sweaty warmth I could smell.

"What the fuck?" I whispered to Helga.

"Sh," she cautioned because of a rippling movement amongst the bodies below. They were so quiet. Too quiet for children their age.

I thought I saw the reason emerge from the kids closest to the fire. An adult in a hooded bathrobe, or a white cloak maybe, removed a bbq cover from something definitely not a bbq.

"What the fuck," Helga said softly.

An iron sarcophagus had been revealed. Sarcophagus might be the wrong word. I only use it because it had the vague shape of a human body and looked made to fit a person inside, albeit a small one. There were no ornaments or paintings of an Egyptian kind or anything.

That's because it's a tool, and its purpose is utilitarian.

The white cloaked person pushed the table over the fire; it moved smoothly as if on wheels.

All the kids stirred and held out bowls and cups if they had them; some put their hands together. They began to beg, "Carn? Carn?" It was a question in a language I didn't know, and it filled the humid garage, a discordant choir of despair.

The cloaked figure threw back his hood, revealing an ancient, bearded man with dark eyes. He lifted his hand and the children went silent.

"Homoni," he answered a moment before a horrid scream erupted from within the sarcophagus The fire had begun to heat the iron. What was inside, animal or human, I couldn't say.

Helga snapped more pictures while I thought of calling the cops.

She read my mind and touched my arm. "Don't," she whispered. "I already tried. They won't come. That's why we're here."

"You've seen this before?"

Helga stopped taking photos to consider me. I've no doubt she wondered if I would run after hearing what she said next. "I've seen what carn is. I saw what comes out of that barbecue coffin. It's meat, and I'm afraid I can guess what kind."

Homoni.

The tortured screams faded and another silence was observed. Bowls and cups and hands were lowered; no meat tonight. Working a sliding rod, the old man released a trap door beneath the sarcophagus. Out fell a gelatinous figure the approximate size of a child.

"It's... is it fat?"

Helga didn't answer but I think she knew. It was fat accumulated from a number of these cookouts. When they had enough, the time to create another Homoni had arrived.

The children watched the fire and some crept forward, but any that got too close were rebuked by the wizard and kicked if they didn't listen.

He opened the top of the sarcophagus next to a dark tangle of charred bones. From the pile, he selected several, including a small ribcage, before bending over the fire and fat. These he arranged on the fat and as it melted, the bones were absorbed.

From his cloak, he produced a bottle and poured the contents onto his creation. A plume of black smoke rose to the hole we spied from. Both of us pulled away to avoid breathing in the unholy vapour.

"Helga, let's go," I told her. "This is clearly fucked."

She nodded, took a step, and dropped right through a soft spot. I reacted fast enough to grab the collar of her coat but her weight pulled me down too, and then a section of roof stripped inward like rotted fabric. We swung high over the ritual and fell together.

Helga broke my fall and saved my life. Too bad it killed her. She'd landed on a pile of scrap metal and old car parts. One look at her spilled skull and I knew. There was no point in checking for signs of life.

I had no time anyway.

Hundreds of sparkling eyes looked at me with childish delight.

"Carn?" said one, and then the rest joined in with certainty.

"Carn! Carn!" They shrieked and raged and poured across the floor like vermin. I leapt backward over Helga and the steel, but they came too fast, scratching with filthy long fingernails and snapping with jagged teeth.

I had no choice.

How many children do you think you could take in a fight?

I discovered the answer that night, and will never be the same. The things I did to survive are too horrible to write. By the end, dozens of them were smashed and killed at my feet. There were many more behind the piles of the dead, but they held off. The wizard had lifted his hand.

The children made way for him as he approached the corner I had wedged myself into. I couldn't stop shaking. There was blood in my eyes but whose?

He smiled as he presented his empty hands. Then, before I could stop him, he pressed his thumb and nail into my forehead. It burned. I seized his wrist but he was already backing away and smiling almost compassionately.

There was movement over his shoulder. From the fire, another child - the homoni - emerged, naked except for a coating of dark liquid dripping off him like sweat. He pointed at me but looked at the wizard.

"Carn?"

The old man nodded. "Carn."

And the children came again, more ferocious and determined than before. I pushed and killed and felt my body weakening as their little hands tore away skin and hair.

Somehow, I made a way through to a door and then I was running.

"Carn!" the children called after me. "Carn! Carn!"

I didn't slow until it became a question again.

"Carn? Carn?"

Only when I'd reached the interior of the tourist district in Bridal Veil Lake did I stop completely. I vomited onto the sidewalk and someone called the police. I didn't stick around. Helga had told them what she'd seen, and they hadn't helped.

I went home, showered, and checked my injuries.

While I could never forget that awful night, I thought at least the ordeal was over.

I was wrong.

The first one knocked on my door a few nights later.

"Carn?" he said like some fucked up trick-or treater. I shut the door but he wouldn't go away. I had no choice. They aren't real kids anyway, right? Homoni.

The next one got in while I was sleeping. I dreamt of ants biting my toes. I'm sure you can guess what I woke up to gnawing on me; lost a baby toe.

"Carn?" it asked after swallowing a piece of me. It's the only fucking word they seem to know.

"Carn?" five asked a few days later as I showered. I got them. I killed them, I mean, but there are teeth marks and a deep grooving gash on the side of my neck that won't heal right.

They kept coming. They keep coming.

I tried staying in a hotel. I even left Bridal Veil Lake for a week.

But nothing has worked.

They come hungry.

They want their meat.

They know how to find me.

What the fuck do I do?

"Oh hello, police? Hordes of cannibal children are hunting me. I've managed to kill them all so far, but I don't know how long I can keep this up. Their bodies?"

Don't ask me about the bodies.

I can't keep them. I can't risk taking them out the front door or burying them in the yard.

They're not human.

Homoni.

Carn.

What's the difference?

They don't see one.

Why should I?

As I write these last words, there are rapid knocks on the door. It's 3:24 AM. There are a dozen, maybe more, on the lawn. Children with empty eyes, underdressed for the cold, and dirty from neglect. This could be it, and I am afraid. I don't want to die. I don't want to know what it'll be like to die this way. They feast before they kill. It seems to be their way, and it's probably why I'm still alive.

I kill first.

But I'm not winning.

"Carn?" I'll ask them and they will ask the same.

Then we'll see who's right.

The Real Reason For Electricity

50%, AND YOU PLUG IT in. 100% gives that feeling of comfort. That phone, that tablet, that laptop, the toaster, your microwave. Why keep the last one plugged in? Because you like the little digital clock on it, the kind found on a five dollar watch that uses way less power and takes up like twenty times less space.

I used to be an environmentalist. I don't know anymore. I certainly don't act like it. Everything in my house is plugged in. I have three microwaves in the kitchen.

Because I know the real reason for electricity.

It's the same as fire, and not what you're thinking.

I know because of what happened in 1999.

We were students at the Joseph Avery College in Bridal Veil Lake, living in the student slum off-campus. Our landlord was pissed off with us because we'd refused to stop throwing parties that were, admittedly, kind of wrecking the house. He wanted us out after Christmas, but we refused. So he stopped paying the hydro bill and we were soon in the dark.

Calling the utilities company would have been the best decision. There are rules against a landlord taking away services considered vital. What we ended up doing, however, was reveling in being closer to a state of nature. Another party to celebrate the dark was held, and we all got very drunk. The house suffered, and we thought it was funny.

Maybe we deserved what happened.

After the party, the darkness and the cold weren't as much fun. We had candles and discussed building a firepit right in the house since there was no fireplace, but Alek pointed out, wisely, that we'd suffocate without a chimney or exhaust of some kind. Using matches and scented candles became tedious and dangerous. Alek also warned us against falling asleep with a lit fire nearby. I guess he was the smartest one.

We began living with the dark, stumbling around in the mess we never cleaned up and staying on campus as much as possible. A few of the guys had girlfriends and convinced them to let them move into their places temporarily.

That left four of us, single losers, to freeze in the dark: Alek, myself, Dan, and Arthur. All of us, except maybe Alek, were best described as side-kicks to one of the guys who'd moved in with their girlfriends.

Alek was the exception; he wasn't a leader either, more a lone wolf who kept to himself except when a house matter concerning him came up or the party was already rolling. The man enjoyed drinking.

With everyone gone, he became our leader by default, a role he did not desire in the slightest.

"We just have to make it till Spring, " he said. "Remember to shower." He went to his room.

Months went by. Batteries for flashlights ran out, and so too our stash of lifted matchbooks from the hotels around Tour Hill. By then, we had changed, not for the better, but neither worse, I would say. Just different. We'd gotten used to traversing the dark and made sure to do certain chores like cleaning and homework during the day.

At night, it became customary for us to gather in the living room and talk. We couldn't see each other, but it was comforting to hear their news of the day and joke around. If we had some money we'd order in pizza and try to guess what kind we were eating by taste alone.

Before the last night in that house, this story would have been a funny anecdote in a different forum, a fond memory spoken of in a few sentences, instead of what it is, what I'm writing now, after all these years of trying to forget.

We sat on the couches, huddled beneath threadbare blankets and wearing all of our clothes. A winter storm actively pounded the house and city outside, the only really significant storm we'd had, and it came in late March. As we discussed upcoming exams and whether or not the snow could be used to insulate the house, we heard a noise, a knocking, in the basement.

It was arrhythmic, intentional, like a morse code hitting the ceiling below. I could feel it in my shivering feet.

"What the hell is that?" Alek asked us all. No one knew, so no one answered. The basement wasn't finished. Just a dusty concrete floor and framing had been done for the owner to update or not at their convenience. Our landlord had mentioned adding rooms, but without a fire exit, kitchen, or bathroom, it'd be illegal.

The knocking continued.

"Think it's an intruder?" Dan asked, the question directed to Alek, our leader. There was a window into the basement.

Alek sighed. He'd been drinking. We all had. "Why don't you find out?" It was a joke, but nobody laughed. In the dark, senses are heightened. No matter how familiar or inebriated, you're always on edge.

I heard Dan stand up. "Fine," he snapped. He stomped his feet from the living room, and we heard him on the creaky basement stairs after feeling the sudden draft from the door we rarely opened. Fresh air wafted in. Maybe that window had been busted open. Maybe the basement was just cold.

For a long time, we sat in silence, listening to the knock and hearing nothing from Dan.

"I call his beer if he's dead," Arthur said, failing to cover the fear with his lameass joke.

"What the hell is he doing down there?" I asked.

"Shut up, listen." Alek stood up and stepped lightly to the adjoining hallway, just outside the threshold of the living room. I knew because of a familiar pop in the hardwood, the one that said the stairs to the second floor were within reach, and the basement was ahead before the kitchen.

I'm sure I heard something, faint whispers or a soft clicking of a tongue coming from the hallway.

"Dan?" Alek asked.

All hell broke loose.

Somebody roared with every fiber of their body, the noise prolonged amidst a collision of bodies culminating in a steady thud against flesh. Bones popped, and Alek groaned.

"What the f-fuck?" I asked.

The noise of the attack continued, subtle wet squishing into tendered meat.

I stood up. "Arthur? Arthur?" He wouldn't answer. The attack stopped, and I either felt hostile eyes upon me or reacted as if they were. The unconscious mind will always err on the side of caution. If danger is possible, best to run. Even if you're wrong, you're still alive.

The other option is to fight. I should have fought. Nobody helped Alek.

The first creak on the floor made me drop, and crawl, squeeze, under the couch by the window. It was a poor hiding spot. Only the darkness made it viable. Hopefully, whoever had come didn't bring a flashlight. My guess is they hadn't been so prepared.

Probably, a thief had seen a darkened house in a storm and assumed no one was home. They broke in the basement, killed Dan, and now killed Alek. Arthur had split already. I might survive if I didn't cross the thief.

But why kill someone you definitely couldn't see? How did they know where Alek had been in the hall? Sweat soaked through my clothes and turned cold. I started to shiver and clenched my teeth so they wouldn't chatter.

For a long time, a very soft smacking was all that could be heard, followed by what may have been someone swallowing.

A footstep on the floor by the coffee table triggered the duct sound below, a flex in a weakened point in the metal. The knocking had stopped. Had that been the thief too? In that case, they wanted to confront the residents before robbing the place. Knocking had been a lure.

Only a psychopath would do that. I felt worse and worse. The invader was searching for targets. That's why they killed Alek. Was Alek dead? Was Dan? Too many stupid questions. Fight or flight? Run or stay like a coward beneath the couch, hoping to survive?

It was so quiet. I allowed small, controlled breaths only. Another footstep followed, padding softly until a tap at the end like the killer went barefoot and had long toenails.

The stench that hit me supported the idea of the invader neglecting his foot hygiene. It was worse than shit, though shit figured greatly in the odor's composition. There was rot and death, a hint of soil, and wet fur.

I drank too much. My gut revolted and I started gagging as vomit filled my mouth. Not enough space under the couch to roll over. I turned my head, and the bile spilled onto my cheek and neck. I started choking.

I pressed the couch and pushed it off my torso so I could twist and clear my throat. The springs or wires or whatever the hell holds a couch together whined with a new weight, pinning my shins. The invader had stepped onto the couch. They made a sound like licking. They were licking their lips?

The slightest gust crossed my nose. A hand swatted the darkness, searching for the next kill. Foul, hot breath filled the narrow space between the back of the couch and the wall.

They were close, mere inches away, somehow poised above, savoring the moment of intense fear gradually withering to acceptance. There was nothing I could do.

"I know you're there," said a quiet voice.

I shut my eyes tight and thought I died when I heard a loud beep from the kitchen. The pressure on the couch relented, and the invader departed leisurely. I heard it going back downstairs.

The hydro had come back on. We'd left so many switches in the on position.

When I opened my eyes, I saw Arthur under the couch opposite. His eyes were wide open, and he had voided his bowels during the ordeal. I thought he might be dead, but saw his chest rise and fall.

What followed felt like the worst kind of awakening. Illuminated, heated, the house seemed noisy and alien. We didn't live there anymore. It'd been too long in the dark.

Streaks of blood led to the open front door, turning to heavy, red droplets on the snowed-in porch, filling the plunging footsteps Alek had left behind. The trail went across the street to a covered pile about the size of his body.

"Arthur," I remember saying a lot. Then we called the police and I sat back down. Firefighters extracted us from the house and brought us to the hospital. I slept a lot there, which surprised me. I thought I'd never sleep again. Each time I awoke, however, it was in panic and terror.

I told my story about a million times to different people, including my parents whose arrival seemed magical. I don't remember when they got to the hospital.

"A cougar broke into the house, son," my dad, in the presence of a constable, said. The story, according to some detective, I suppose, was that the starving cougar had entered through the basement window. Dan had been found at the bottom of the stairs, dead from a fall.

His death had almost nothing to do with the animal. He'd slipped in the dark and hit his head. The cougar, for some reason, had missed his body and came upstairs, where it attacked Alek, pulling his arm off. Since the limb wasn't found, like the cougar itself, it was assumed to be eaten, bone and all.

Alek had been found under the snow, where I thought. He was trying to get help from the neighbors but died of blood loss on their lawn, buried by the storm.

When the hydro came on, the cougar fled back through the window it'd come through. The landlord had apparently paid the bill prior to the storm, worried he'd be liable if we died. Everything had turned on when it did by chance.

There are a number of problems with this convenient explanation, which I'm sure anyone reading this can notice. I'll list a few of the major inconsistencies:

No tracks or prints from the cougar were found in or outside the house. Snow, apparently, filled the exterior ones. A shrug is the explanation for the lack inside; it just didn't leave a single one on the hardwood. Seems, at best, unlikely.

Second, cougars this far south in Ontario are unheard of. While there have been sightings, few have ever been confirmed. I could only find one news story about a cougar entering a home, and that wasn't in this province.

Moreover, the cougar that supposedly attacked us hasn't been seen or tracked since. The obvious place to look would be the western gorge in Bridal Veil Lake. To my knowledge, nobody has bothered to search.

The biggest, but by no means the last problem with the cougar explanation, is what I know I heard the invader say:

I know you're there

It hadn't been Arthur. He can't remember much. Like me, he never really recovered, but he's adamant he never said a word, though he didn't hear anyone either.

"Why would I say something like that?" he quite reasonably asked the one time we were interviewed together.

It wasn't his voice.

I know.

It was a voice, however, and cougars don't talk. A hungry predator wouldn't bypass an easy meal - Dan - and wouldn't flee because some lights came on.

I know better. Arthur does too. We gave each other generators for Christmas and piles of batteries on our birthdays.

It's not the light it fears. It's the order, it's the warmth of civilization granted by electricity and fire. The way we're attracted to a lit hearth and turn on music to disturb the silence repels it.

You turn off your lights and make your house quiet for a night. Nothing wrong with that.

But there's a reason you have trouble sleeping with all the power out.

You just might not realize what it is yet.

They Make Them Cry

CHILD ACTORS, ALL GROWN up, never talk about it.

I'm not sure if they remember.

I feel like part of them must, and that's why people catch their latent anxiety and think they're messed up on drugs.

It's very rare for a child actor to bridge the gap to adult acting. And I think those that do must have been very lucky. They never had a role requiring the Daughters of Eris.

That's not what they call themselves.

The Daughters of Eris, according to my quick internet search, come from Greek mythology. They were like minor gods responsible for sorrow and weeping, I think.

I looked it up back in 2010 because I'd just started as a production assistant for a minor film company out of Toronto. Essentially, my boss, a chain smoking asshole I barely saw, got contracts to send equipment and assistants like me to bigger studios from America.

There's a rule about the percentage of Canadian workers on a set. If a company met that percentage, they were entitled to tax benefits and sometimes funding too.

It doesn't matter beyond the reason why a twenty-something kid out of film school should suddenly be walking around a set doing fetch quests for just about everyone else. Literally, I was the bottom rung of a very long ladder, and took a lot of abuse for only decent money.

Lots of free food though.

Right, so I looked up the Daughters of Eris because some dude said I needed to clear and reserve a room for them in this old, huge house we were filming a scary movie in.

Sorry, I can't tell you which one. I'm scared to share this story already. I don't know what's going to happen once they find this post on reddit. Hopefully, they never do.

I'm only writing this because I feel like people should know: Don't put your kids in the movies, especially if it's a drama or something requiring tears.

Film people are often fucked up. It seems to be a requirement for advancement in the industry. Like the higher you go, the more self-important and crazy you must be. Here are some examples:

I watched a rather famous director, after the incident I'm writing about today, literally walk onto set with a shoebox full of cocaine. Don't worry, it was to share. He was upset when I didn't want any, and made me leave the production. This is considered totally reasonable within the industry.

Another very famous director once punched out another production assistant when a camera stopped working and a difficult shot failed. The production assistant went to the hospital with black eyes and a concussion. The director went back to work and finished the film. You almost certainly know the film and probably saw it. That director is a billionaire now, and his movies suck.

The point is these people do not care about humans. Actors, assistants, and everyone occupy the same level of importance as props and tools. All have been supplied to make a vision of extreme importance in the mind of a few disturbed people.

I used to really love movies. Now I just can't.

Not that I know what is done for the most convincing performances.

The Daughters of Eris only send one agent to a set. Nobody gets to see them. Nobody but the actor they've been contracted to work with. Not even the godlike directors stay; it's about the only time the lofty film folk are sobered up through an almost tangible apprehension.

See, employing the Daughters of Eris is a risky move. It can make or destroy a film, a career, a life. Only the most intense assholes on the planet - those so deep in the industry and into their own rear ends

- have heard of them and then still gone on to sign their nefarious contracts.

Again, the Daughters of Eris is not what they call themselves. It's a name industry insiders, the deeply cloistered ones, gave them in the sixties. They actually have no names other than what humanity has whispered in the dark for centuries.

You might not know what primal fear is, but I can explain: it's the dread you feel when there's a sound you can't identify and everything else, every other sense, is prevented by pitch black night. It's both the unknown and the inability to act to resolve the situation. No light within reach. No pets in the house to reasonably blame. Nothing can be done except passively waiting for what's to come, and hoping nothing does.

"Room one. Ready?" That's the way they talk to a production assistant. Nevermind the one asking was also a production assistant. Dave had been there for years and been fully converted to the lifestyle.

"Ready? No," I confessed, "I just emptied it. I was about to see what the instructions were for furnishings and-"

Dave spoke fast into his headset. "It's ready. Bring the kid. Clear the set."

The kid in question we'll call Bella both to protect her identity and to hopefully pass along the beauty and the innocence of her. She looked scared. Her mom pulled Bella by her forearm roughly.

"Hey-"

Dave got in my face and started pushing my shoulders. "Set needs to be clear. Out." When I saw Bella's mom leave the basement with some other crew members - fast - and Dave passed me by the front door of the house, I stopped.

"What about Bella? What's going on?"

Dave tried to grab my wrist through the threshold, reluctant to come back inside. I pulled away.

"What about the kid? Who's down there with her?"

The look in Dave's eyes as he shook his head and took off said it all: the kid was alone.

"The hell with that." I didn't give a shit what anybody said. I pushed through the fleeing remnants on my way to the basement. Happily, I would be sent home and off the production and they could shove their stupid horror movie up their ass.

I don't know what I expected to see when I got down there. Certainly, the room had been made to look like a colonial stone-aged leftover, the kind a cult would approve of, with its crude altar, cobwebs, and corners darkened amidst a carefully prepared clutter of everyday things. Yet, the lone girl, dressed in the cliche white nightdress, seated on the bare floor, still made me uneasy.

Nothing besides recording cameras and bright lights filled the space. Everyone else had fucked off like a firedrill.

"Bella," I started to say, but the bad feelings grew as I went down the stairs. I felt so bad, I could no longer stand. Fuck, I couldn't even sit right. I tried but ended up stretched out on the floor, covering my head with my hands.

I couldn't speak. The air pressed down, cold and penetrating. Wooden steps creaked with a heavy weight as the Daughter descended. She brought the stench of disease, a vile odor like too much sweat, cloying, stinging, filling my mouth and turning my stomach.

Bella whimpered.

From the ground, I could only see her bare feet, and neatly folded hands. My vision blurred.

Thick legs jammed into undersized shoes. Black tights under strips of cloth that danced in an airless scene.

Bella's whimpering turned to sobs. "No," she said softly.

"Get away from her," I choked out at an even lower volume. I didn't know what was happening, but, as scared as I was, I couldn't live with myself if I didn't try to help.

My first attempt to move didn't prove too fruitful. I sort of spasmed and my arm shot out above my head, painfully scraping across the floor. Bella's scream sounded painful. Adrenaline shot through my veins. I did a slow, shaky push-up and staggered to my feet. The stench continued to make my head swim. I wiped my eyes and could see a little better.

"Get the fuck away from her," I finally managed at an audible level.

The figure ahead had a very wide set of shoulders. What I thought were tendrils were actually tattered coat tails. Tights weren't tights but just tight dress pants. It was a man, a very strange, and disturbing man.

He exhaled and turned around slowly, revealing a severely disfigured face: no nose there. Just a single ragged hole for a nostril that didn't work. His wide mouth hung open and that's how he breathed. Both eyes were milky white, blind, I think. The left side of his face looked like melted wax, scarred in waves of skin. All of his teeth were missing when he smiled.

I couldn't get a straight look at him. His edges were blurry. My eyes kept trying to bring him into focus and the effort made me woozy.

Bella cupped her hands to her face and wept.

"Get...away..." I said again, quietly.

His smile grew and he reached for me with fingers like cigarette lighters, the kind they used to put in old cars and every kid burned themselves on.

I could hardly stand. Fighting, running were out of the question. That left one option. I threw my body into the mounted camera, and managed to crash the lens away from the scene.

I don't know what I thought would result from this action exactly. Some vague idea about ending the shot and thus the frightening ordeal, I guess. Fortunately, it worked. At least, it worked for me.

When I recovered enough to separate from the camera, the blurred man was gone. I don't know if he simply left or disappeared. And I didn't care. He was gone and that was enough.

Bella continued to cry, softer now. I went to her, and gently pulled her hands away to see what had been done. Ashes had been traced in two lines in the center of her forehead. No visible wound had been inflicted but she winced when I wiped the marks away with my sleeve.

I held her until the crew and her shitty mom returned. The assistant director started yelling at me almost immediately and threatened my job. I didn't care. I left the basement without a word, intending to go and never come back.

Instead, I went to the room I had prepared for the Daughters of Eris. I smelled the burnt candles before I saw them. A pentagram had been burned into the floor and there were some red dots that were probably blood.

Some high school looking shit, if I'm being honest.

I left and called my boss.

I wasn't fired, though, I was taken off this stupid film, and I didn't quit. I had mixed feelings for sure and I was pretty fucked up from the ordeal. Had some nightmares about the man that were bad enough to wake me up. Just like in the movies.

But I also had bills to pay.

After a few days off, my boss had me do some other production with no children. Seemed like a prudent choice on his part.

The dumb spooky film didn't make it to release. It happens sometimes, but I still felt bad for Bella. She'd been scarred for nothing. I quit the business a year and a half later and life moved on.

I hadn't thought much about her again until the moment I saw my old boss' number on my phone. He had bad news. Last week, Bella - all of twenty-two - was found in her motel room apartment. She'd overdosed on a cocktail of drugs. Her life, after that stupid unfinished movie, went awfully. My boss never told me until this call that the reason the production collapsed was Bella.

She'd become distracted, inconsolable often, and, at least in one incident, violent. Her mother said the attack was unprovoked. While sitting on set, eating lunch, Bella threw a punch straight into the nose of her terrible mother, breaking it.

Good. At least she got some consequences.

Not so good: Bella was sent to live with her even worse father.

From there, my boss lost what little connection to her he had until he saw her on Tour Hill in Bridal Veil Lake. He was on his way to the casino. She was on her way to work apparently. He recognized her despite the many years that had gone by. She, of course, had no idea who he was but after he explained, she agreed to let him buy her a drink.

Things got weird from there. My old boss got really vague about the details during the phone call. In any case, he knew where she'd been living and became familiar with the owner. That's who called him when Bella died.

The funeral was yesterday. I went. So did the man without a nose. It rained hard yesterday, and everyone had an umbrella. Everyone but him. He stood away, by some trees, and stared, not at the funeral but at me.

I tried to call him out but couldn't hear my own voice in the downpour. The closer I got, the wider his empty smile grew. He wore the same clothes. In fact, he looked exactly the same, right down to the blurred edges, which I don't believe came from the heavy rain affecting my vision.

I also felt the same weakness. I had to stop moving toward him.

He tilted his head as if to ask, "What's wrong?" Then he laughed and that was a terrible thing to hear: guttural and tongueless, but loud enough to make me flinch.

I screamed and finally gained some attention from the other attendees. My old boss wrapped an arm around my shoulder but I shrugged him off.

"He was here," I said, loudly. "The Daughter of Eris."

He just looked nervous. "They never leave the ones that cry."

I noticed everyone purposely not looking at us or the man. When I turned to accost him again, he was gone. Of course.

At a loss as to how I could honor Bella or avenge her even, I wrote this account so that people might reconsider putting their kids into showbiz.

Don't. Just don't. Please.

That's the best I can do, Bella. I'm too afraid to go after the Daughters of Eris myself and really want to leave the ordeal behind.

I am afraid the man will soon pay me a visit. Inside, outside a nightmare, I don't know which is worse.

Goodbye Bella. Rest in peace.

It Wasn't Grimace In The Playplace

I'M AN ANXIOUS FATHER. I never denied it and yes, it did tick off my wife and ruin my daughters' good time on occasion.

But I was right about the playplace at our local McDonald's.

Bridal Veil Lake, like any tourist town, has a lot of restaurants but only one of these burger-toy depositories. Vacationers, I guess, don't want to visit the same old chain when they're away from home.

Most patrons, maybe all, at the McDonald's are locals. It's always an eclectic mix of characters. There are people like me - normal, average, with a job and family - and the rest: people that come to the place daily for cheap sustenance and air conditioning.

I hate McDonald's. I hate fast food. I especially hate that my kids seem to talk about nothing else. My wife used to blame me. By trying to forbid it, I inevitably made it desirable. I don't know if that's true but I can't dispute they always pushed to come - even after the traumatic incident of our first visit.

They were in the playplace - if you aren't aware, many McDonald's have small indoor playgrounds of suspicious cleanliness.

Climbing structures form a three story maze of padded levels, sealed in plastic netting to prevent falling. A tube slide connects the top to the bottom.

I blame my wife - let's call her Zelda - for making me exit the structure and then the playplace room altogether.

"You keep too close," she said. "You're gonna pass on your anxiety. Is that what you want? What your mother did to you?"

We were sitting in one of those simple booths designed to be uncomfortable, so customers would eat and not linger. I could see the playplace through an interior window. I didn't answer my wife because the crowd of children inside started screaming and swarmed toward the exit.

I wasn't the only parent to rush over. My youngest daughter - Dana - came out first, her four-year-old body pushing open the heavy door while a throng of kids jostled behind her. Dana seemed calmer than the others, including her six-year-old sister, Kara, who was crying.

"What's going on?"

Parents scooped up kids. I did the same - one in each arm - and took them back to the booth. A confused looking manager went into the playplace to investigate.

"It was Grimace," Dana said, while Kara sobbed into Zelda's shoulder. "He's a boy and he was chasing us. And he got the other boy who had a blue shirt."

I remember Kara looking at me when a man walked out of the bathroom. He saw the empty playplace and that all the kids were with their parents.

"Cameron!" he called and every parent knew his fear. I went with him into the playplace where a few employees had gathered. The father screamed and searched, jamming his adult body through the structure, looking in every blind spot for his kid. "Cameron!"

There really aren't many places to hide in a playplace.

"Call the police," I told the employees. They did and wisely locked and guarded the doors so no one could leave. The father ran all through the restaurant, including the kitchen and woman's bathroom, and they let him. A manager went to review security footage.

Some patrons complained and protested having to stay put but not me. I would absolutely not let a single one of them out if there was a chance they knew something about my missing child.

The police arrived and took control of the scene. We were asked a few questions. Dana repeated her story about Grimace and the boy in the blue shirt. The father of the boy - Cameron - stared at us when we were allowed to leave.

"That was crazy," Zelda said. I agreed but didn't say more. As usual, I was angry when something bad happened after being told to "relax" my anxieties. I never said, "told you so," but she knew that's how I felt.

Zelda comes from a privileged background. When I talk about growing up where I did, in relative poverty, she doesn't understand. Maybe she can't relate or thinks I'm exaggerating when I tell her, "There are bad people in the world. Like really, really bad, evil people. They're never going to find that boy alive."

Zelda admonished me. "Why would you say something like that? The girls don't need that kind of negativity."

Another minor argument began and never got resolved because we both fell asleep putting our kids to bed in their respective rooms.

I won't bother you with the struggles and nuances of our relationship. It doesn't matter.

I was right. She was wrong. We never should have gone back to McDonald's.

But we did. After months of waiting for news about the missing kid and not getting any, Zelda convinced me it must be fine.

"No news is good news," she said smugly.

"Some news is too horrible to report," I countered, but she just rolled her eyes. "If they're in there, then I am too."

"Fine," she relented.

And lied apparently. The girls had already gone into the playplace before I'd finished ordering their Happy Meals.

"What the hell?" I accused Zelda.

"What?"

Like a nightmare, the scene unfolded the same. Kids screamed and rushed to the exit. There were more than last time. I couldn't see my girls. I pushed through two other dads and the last of the fleeing children.

Outside the window, the clouds were so dark. It was supposed to rain and storm - that's one of the reasons we'd come. It's the only indoor playground in town that doesn't cost hundreds of dollars each visit.

The interior of the playplace looked grim with too many shadows and no one playing.

"Girls?!"

Zelda came with a manager who looked ready to throw up.

"Police are coming. We've locked the doors." The defeated tone told me they never did find Cameron.

"Girls!" I shouted louder. "Girls!" I climbed the first level of the structure.

"Daddy," Dana said, her voice altered by the interior of the tube slide.

"Dana," I said, slightly relieved. The feeling was less than brief, however.

"Don't come in here, daddy," she said. "Grimace will-"

Another scream and I knew it came from Kara.

"Daddy," Dana said again, but pleadingly.

I ran through the narrow corridors designed for under ten and bashed my head and tripped over stupid obstacles along the path. Cursing, I crawled into the tube slide head first and immediately felt the wrongness of the space.

For one, my ample dad bod slid along too easily, as if sucked through a crazy straw. Two, the ride was longer than possible. I kept winding around the twists and the air became colder as the remnants of ambient light were left behind and above.

And three, it was too quiet. Even the sound of my short, panicked breaths seemed muted by the darkness ahead.

I lost my sense of direction and place in the world. I could be moving or not. There was nothing to see or feel to know for sure.

I turned on my cell flashlight and found Dana's sweaty, scared little face looking back at me. Neither of us were sliding anymore.

When I reached for her, she squirmed away.

"No daddy," she said, "Grimace got Kara. I have to get her." She tried to go further down the slide and it only occurred to me then that we should still be moving. The steep angle and gravity said so. Yet, we were stuck.

I grabbed her tiny four-year-old arm and pulled her into my lap. She fought but I wouldn't let go.

"I will get Kara," I told her.

"I need to come too," she said, resisting less, and patting my hand.

"Why?"

"Grimace is strong," she said. "and he hides really good from adults."

I was about to start pushing her back up the slide. Losing one child breaks any father. Losing both is a horror of unknown depths. I couldn't fathom such a calamity. My body took over. I started shoving amidst her protests, and then another pair of feet appeared above.

"Zelda," I said, "what are you doing?"

She looked like she didn't understand the question.

"Take Dana. I have to get Kara."

She didn't budge. "I'm coming."

There would be no argument. I tried anyway but she shut that shit down fast with a simple appeal: "We don't have time for this. Move!"

So all three of us began our descent, me cursing in a volume directly related to our collective apprehension. All of us shivered; the temperature in the tube had dropped. The plastic sides were coated with a thin layer of frost.

I don't know how long we were dragging ourselves before Zelda and I shared the terror in our eyes.

"This can't be happening," she said. "It's a nightmare. We're not really here." She wrung her hands. "We're not really here." She closed her eyes. "We're not really here."

For obvious reasons, Zelda had lost her shit. I struggled hard to get to her. The slide resumed utility when I tried going up. In retrospect, it was like it wanted us not to move or to at least slow us down.

Dana got to her first. She put her hand on top of Zelda's. "It's happening, mommy, and it's okay. But we have to hurry." The resolve of this kid drew away some of the fear, enough to get us moving again.

The light app on my cell noticeably dimmed. I looked at the screen. Only fifteen percent power remained. I'd charged it to one hundred before coming to McDonald's.

"Zelda," I said, "my phone is dying. Do you-"

She pulled it from her pocket and passed it over without hesitation. I entered the password - we use the same - and her browser was open. One word had been typed into the search bar: divorce.

I closed the browser, found the flashlight, and resumed moving with a growing numbness beneath the primal fear surging through my body. I had to save Kara. That's all that mattered now.

Divorce.

What a damned place to find out.

With my extreme, often unreasonable levels of anxiety, I'm not an easy person to live with, let alone love. So Zelda wanting to leave wasn't a surprise. More like an unavoidable outcome, sooner than expected, but not shocking. Everyone gets tired of me eventually.

At last, we came to it, the end, but not. What blocked the path of the slide is best described as gelatinous goo, purple, and with a kind of face. More like the suggestion of a face. Imagine a child dragging three of their fingers through a splash of thick paint to make eyes, a mouth, and nothing more.

At last, we found Grimace. His "face" filled the entire cylinder.

"Jesus Christ," Zelda said between hyperventilated breaths.

Dana pointed over my shoulder. "That's Grimace," she said. "He ate Kara, and the other boy." She sounded older than four.

"Kara," I said, "is in there?" I didn't know what "in there" meant. Beyond there? Inside there? Inside it? "What... the... fuck..." This can't be happening. Zelda's mantra threatened to burst from my lips.

We were in a fucking, stupid McDonald's playplace. What the fuck was this? And where were we?

This can't be happening.

I resisted looking at my soon to be ex, afraid I would lose what little remained of my composure. Dana shivered so hard against my back.

"Kara?" I called.

The mouth parted to reveal only more purple goo within. It was fucking smiling.

I tried to jab my index finger in the air toward it, but my fear made the digit wobble. The gesture looked pathetic. Nevertheless, I spoke. "Give... her back... you..."

From its abyss came the laughter of the damned, a desperate, hopeless ringing that said, "I have nothing to lose." Sad that I know what that sounds like.

"Give her back."

More laughter.

"Give. Her. Back!" I plunged my hands into its face, penetrating with surprising ease. That streak of a smile inverted. I was pleased by its sudden dismay.

So cold though. I've never felt so cold.

Zelda and Dana were shouting. I couldn't distinguish their words from one another.

I had everything to lose. I went head first down the slide, pressing the top of my head into Grimace's visage. With a deep breath, I crawled all the way through, plunging into a dark space lit dully by Zelda's phone.

There were no walls or edges to this void. Yet, Kara's pink, unicorn sock rested on a surface, even if I couldn't see it. I tried to crouch in order to stand up but my head hit something hard. It was like I was still inside the tube slide.

The bottom of Kara's small foot rested at the edge of yet another shadow. Small droplets of dark, purple goo dripped from somewhere unseen. I smelled burnt hair before I realized the liquid was acidic. If Kara had been here for long...

In a daze, in pain, I scrambled for her, and grasped her leg, pulling as hard as I could. She emerged as if stuck in the dark. I pulled her small body into my lap and saw the trouble.

In her grasp she held a blue shirt, a child's shirt, and inside the sleeve were the decaying bones of a child. No, not decaying. Digested. Kara had found the missing boy. She had found Cameron, or what was left of him.

I shrieked as I tried to free Kara's fingers from the shirt, but she wouldn't let go. As I shook her forearm, Cameron's remains disintegrated into something like sand. I gave up and clumsily rolled and maneuvered until facing the theoretical interior of Grimace's face.

It looked much the same as the exterior.

The only difference was that it wasn't smiling, and it wasn't dismayed. Grimace was pissed. Its facsimile features swirled fiercely and we were spun a few times through the acidic soup trailing from its innards. It burned and I screamed. Kara wasn't conscious but she moaned.

I dropped Zelda's phone. The light slipped and jostled below where I thought the way was horizontal. The face of Grimace was actually higher than us.

For a moment, I knew where to place my feet for leverage. I retrieved the phone and squirmed through the burning goo and punched through its cheek. Kara almost slipped from my left arm.

There was nothing on the other side to grab hold of. His suggestion of a face became placidly supreme again. But only for a moment. Strong hands on the other side found mine. Zelda and Dana pulled us through while I writhed to get free.

"Die," the fucking monster rasped. Its gooey face began to lurch like a bloated snail toward us.

"Quick! Run!" Dana shrieked. Her tiny body fit perfectly in the slide. She could bend her head and brace her shoulders against the top. That allowed her to move upwards pretty fast. Zelda and I, obviously, had less suited proportions.

"Go!" I shouted at her, shoving Kara into her embrace. She hesitated. I handed her the phone. "Go," I said with quiet resolve. "It's okay. I get it. It's okay. I know what I have to do."

"Dear, I-"

I felt its liquid mouth glom onto the heel of my sneaker. "It's okay. Go. I'll see you up there." Thankfully, she relented and took the only light away. As predicted, "Grimace" slowed down as he began to consume me. I didn't struggle. Frankly, it was a relief to just give up and not have to worry anymore.

"What are you?" I asked.

It answered with its mouth full... of me. "I am exactly what you were afraid of all along, a messenger, here to validate your belief: there are no safe and innocent places. Aren't you happy? You were right. You. Were. Right."

I had been swallowed up to the waist. The acid interior began to burn, but I didn't scream. If I did, Zelda or the girls or all of them together might come back.

The pain became unbearable. I started to struggle, which made it chuckle. Getting out proved easier than before. Yet, I only delayed the inevitable. The slimey sound of its ponderous pursuit resumed.

"You could run," it said, "but you know there's nowhere I can't find you. Or your children. Or maybe your wife."

"Fuck you."

It laughed and its gelatinous bile touched again. Quickly, I pulled my feet away and touched the exposed toe bone. The acid had eaten my shoe, sock, and a fair amount of skin.

Panic overcame the exhaustion of my continual anxiety. I crawled away, upward, slowly. The frosted interior warmed and I fell from the mouth of the slide.

Zelda held my head in her lap. Kara had awakened. While there were reddened marks on her skin, she seemed okay. She was alive more importantly.

In her hands, she clutched Cameron's blue shirt.

The creature defied rationality. How could the acid consume my shoe and sock but only the bones of the boy?

Unless... it could control its own digestion. It wanted to save the shirt. Like a serial killer, it wanted a keepsake of the murder, a trophy.

"What is it? What is it? What is it?" Someone frantically asked over and over. It wasn't until I heard Zelda's voice that I realized it was me. I'd finally lost it, and my thoughts departed until something far worse, a greater fear, brought me down to reality.

"You were right, dear," Zelda said, "there is evil. I should have listened. You. Were. Right."

And I'd never wanted to be more wrong in my whole entire life. The creature had won. We both believed in it and its residency in the places where children were supposed to play and be safe.

A cocky teenager went down the slide to prove its safety, to defy my rantings about a monster. He laughed at me when he popped out the other side.

Doctors concluded the injuries I'd received and Kara's were due to extreme friction. They didn't say it, but I believe they thought I had done this to myself and my daughter.

Zelda didn't file for divorce.

We didn't go back to McDonald's.

We never went anywhere unless we had to, and the creature's power only grew until even necessary places - grocery stores, the doctor, school - became filled with our ceaseless fears of the potential evil that could be there.

If only there'd been no little blue shirt. It existed. We kept it. Did it prove the existence of Grimace? No. But it made it impossible to forget what had happened in the slide.

"Dad," Dana asked the other day, "can we go outside?"

I stared at her.

Zelda answered. "Honey, no, we talked about this. Your father was right, remember?" She gripped my forearm. "We will never forget: He was right about the world.

I Want To Go Outside

I SAW THE TIME ON THE digital clock: 2:59 AM.

I rolled over and went back to sleep.

That's why we were having a sleepover at Pilar's house.

Bobby woke up at 2:59 AM, and did what I had, what any sane person would.

Only Pilar had seen 2:59 AM and thought to get out of bed.

"I saw him," he said the next day. We met in the middle of our street - Ferry Street - on our bikes. It was 1990 in mid August, and we were ten. The apprehension and wonder of the new middle school we would enter had been totally numbed by the death of our fathers.

They'd died in the same accident the previous March. Our fathers were close and moved to Ferry Street at the same time. After a few drinks at the pub, they were walking home. The drunk driver didn't realize he'd taken them out with his truck. He kept going, parked in his driveway, and passed out in his car.

When he called 911, the next day, he said somebody had been murdered on his car. Pilar, Bobby, and I were at the funeral, and didn't understand exactly what had happened.

Our fathers were gone. Our moms became so fragile. We were on our own. We only had each other. It wasn't enough.

We went through the motions of friendship and life, and couldn't express the loss. Even now, the best I can do is to suggest it was like going to a funeral every day without visiting the cemetery. Without burying a body.

People gave us pained looks and offered their condolences. We didn't know what that meant, and had no way of looking it up.

Pilar called it bullshit. Bobby got quieter and seemed always on the verge of tears. I don't know what I became other than something hollow.

"We all woke up at 2:59 AM," Pilar said.

"How do you know that?" I asked.

He shrugged. "I... don't know... but I'm right, aren't I? Listen, guys, our dads... they're back. I saw them last night. They were walking up the road at three."

Bobby and I shared an incredulous look.

"No, really, guys, I can prove it. Stay over tonight. You'll see." There was no point in asking our moms for permission. In these dark times, they agreed to everything without really hearing what we said.

I asked anyway. "Is it okay to sleep at Pilar's tonight?"

"Sure, sure," my mom said. She was in bed. I don't know if she got up that day.

Pilar set us up in his living room. His place looked pretty dirty. There were empty beer bottles everywhere. I think he'd been drinking them. He seemed kind of tired and his eyes were half-lidded.

We played video games on his old TV, and had snacks for dinner. Close to eleven, I started to yawn.

"Tired?" Pilar asked us both.

"Yup," Bobby said. His usual patience had grown thin. Maybe he thought Pilar's scheming had finally crossed a line. I found it comforting.

Pilar had endless exaggerated tales before our dads died. They'd ended at the funeral.

Now they seemed to be back. I didn't know how he knew we'd all awakened at the same time. And I didn't think I'd see my dad. But the return of his lies felt like the normalcy I so desperately needed.

"Pillows are upstairs," Pilar said, observing that neither of us had brought any. After a moment pondering how I could forget a pillow, I trudged up to the second floor and noted further degradation in the house.

Pilar's mom had trashed the place, and never cleaned up. There were slashes in the wallpaper and smashed frames. All the lights were off but we knew the place well, having stayed over countless times before.

I heard his mom snoring through her open bedroom door. Wisely, I kept moving and found the pillows. Scant light from outside put a portrait around a red mark on his dresser. I had put it there. Pilar and I were blood brothers.

Bobby had declined the ritual after seeing me freak out over my bloody thumb. I'd used the dresser handle to pull myself up before I booked it home, crying all the way.

I returned to the living room to find Pilar settling into his spot on the couch. Bobby sat on his sleeping bag.

"Did you set an alarm or something?" I asked.

Pilar smiled. "No need. We'll wake up. Don't worry." He yawned.

Bobby rolled his eyes and turned on the Nintendo. He didn't have video games at home, so he would spend the night in a way he found worthwhile. It might have been the only reason he'd endured Pilar's tale about 2:59 AM.

I picked up the second controller and entered the Konami code for Contra; the sequence of buttons was prized lore among kids. It gave the extra lives needed to complete difficult games. Bobby smiled but looked sad and exhausted.

"You okay, Bobby?"

He didn't answer the objectively stupid question. "Think we could beat this without cheating? Do you think anyone has? Like... you get so few lives without the cheat code... it isn't fair. It isn't." Bobby shook his head and his little gun toting avatar died when he took his hand off the controller to wipe his tears.

"You're right," I said. "It isn't fair."

We played for a few hours and agreed to sleep, believing strongly in the possibility that Pilar would wake us up at 2:59 in order to do something stupid.

"I love him, you know," Bobby said. "And I fucking hate his guts." We were both in our sleeping bags, staring at the white ceiling.

"Pilar?" I asked, but Bobby didn't answer. I figured he went to sleep, so I did the same.

2:59 AM came next.

"Look! Look! Get ready!" Pilar shouted until we were fully awake. "They're coming! Hurry!" He beckoned us over to the wide window behind the couch.

The street outside had never been brightly lit. I saw a man staggering alone, a drunken shadow that could be anyone. To my surprise, I was disappointed. I wanted it to be true.

"Pilar, man, I mean, come on," I said.

"No, wait, just wait," he said.

I humoured him and kept watching. A shaft of unnatural light Illuminated his face. He looked straight at me from the middle of the road and smiled as if it had all been a mistake. I couldn't believe it. My dad stood there, alive and well - and a little drunk.

"Dad!" Bobby shouted. "Dad!" He scrambled off the couch and tripped over the coffee table. "Wait! Just wait! I'm coming!"

I looked back outside. It was my dad there.

Pilar started next. "Dad! Dad!" He went for the front door. Instantly, I knew, all of it was wrong.

"No! Stop! Stop!" But they didn't. Both were fighting one another to unlock the door. I bowled into them. They had to see reason: we couldn't all be seeing our fathers in one man.

"Stop!" I shouted, blocking the now unlocked door. "There's one guy out there. I saw my dad. And you saw yours. That isn't possible!"

"Get out of the way!" Bobby yelled, grabbing my arms and pulling. Pilar joined him. Together, they overpowered me, and opened the door, admitting a rush of cold air and silence unnatural to an August night in Bridal Veil Lake.

I grabbed at both but knew I could only hold one. I chose the blood brother. Bobby sprinted down the walkway to whatever the hell waited outside. I saw the shadow kneel and open its arms. Its face gone, indistinct in the dark, and certainly not any of our fathers.

Pilar and I fell to the floor. I managed to entangle him and kick shut the door. When I did, we both heard the anguished cry from Bobby. A strangled, futile plea followed, which made Pilar and I look at one another.

"He's gone," Pilar said. "He's gone. Oh my god."

I pushed him away. I opened the door and it was true. The man - the thing that had appeared as my father and Pilar's and Bobby's - was gone. So was Bobby. No sign of either remained.

The unusual quiet ceased, and the night resumed its cadence of crickets and traffic in the distance.

I went inside. My hands were trembling but I felt detached from the world and my body.

"You saved me," Pilar said flatly. He closed the door, and reached over my shoulder to lock it. He went into the living room and found his sleeping bag. Somehow, he rolled over and went to sleep.

I didn't know what to do.

I sat on the floor. When bad things happened, I used to go to my parents. It's not that our moms didn't care. They couldn't anymore. Too much had happened.

That's why I did nothing too. There was nobody to tell. If I tried, I predicted only more absent-minded acknowledgement that I had spoken.

"Bobby's gone," I'd say.

"Sure, sure," mom would say, and I'd still be on my own. I still wouldn't know what to do. I don't know right now, and it's thirty-four years after the fact. Guess that's why I'm writing about it.

I left Pilar's at the first sign of dawn and found sleep as easily as he had. When I woke up, it was late in the afternoon. I ate waffles for supper and played Nintendo into the night. I didn't see my mom. When I heard her crying, I closed the door.

Bobby's mom didn't call the police. She didn't come to our place or Pilar's to look for him.

Sleeping that night was difficult. I stared out the window, and the digital clock on my nightstand. I had no intention of staying up until 2:59 AM but that's what I did.

At 2:45 AM, Pilar left his house, and crossed the street to mine. He had a coil of rope and a baseball bat.

He knocked on the door rapidly and shouted my name.

I ran downstairs, worried he'd wake up my mom. "What the hell, man?" It felt weird to talk. I hadn't said a word since the previous night.

"Dude!" he yelled, "open the door! I got a plan!"

I reached for the doorknob but hesitated and looked at my hand for no good reason. "Why do you have rope and a bat, Pilar?"

"What?" he asked. "I can barely hear you. Open the door!"

"Pilar," I said, "why do you have that stuff with you?"

He didn't say anything straight away, and then, "We're gonna get that thing! We're gonna get Bobby back! Come on!"

I could picture Bobby rolling his eyes.

Another wacky scheme by Pilar.

"Man," I said, "I... can't." I didn't have it in me to face whatever we'd seen last night, and I didn't think a rope, bat or nuclear bomb would be enough to bring Bobby back. He was gone. He is gone. Pilar must have known.

"What? Are you kidding? Bobby..."

"Bobby's gone," I said. "They're all gone. Nobody's coming back. Go home Pilar."

His bat crashed against the door.

"Open the fucking door!"

"Pilar! What the-"

He swung again, and again. The handle rattled on my side as he began to target it.

"Stop!"

"It's coming! Open up! Don't leave me out here, man!"

"Fine! Stop! Okay!"

I might have opened it then but the unnatural quiet consumed the night as it had before. I could hear Pilar whispering, though, not exactly what he said.

"Who are you talking to?" I asked.

"Hurry! He's coming! Hurry!" He resumed his attack on the door, and I almost gave in, I really did, but something occurred to me.

"You didn't go out to see our dads the first night," I said.

"What?"

"Why didn't you go see your dad, Pilar?"

Nothing from the other side for a moment. "Let me in." His tone changed from pleading to anger. "Open the fucking door. Right now!"

I waited. He smashed the handle. I gripped it in mine, willing the door to hold. "You fought me last night, Pilar, but not that hard. He said he loved you. Bobby loved you, Pilar. But you lied about that first night."

"Do you love me?" he asked. "Do you?!"

I thought about my bloody thumbprint. "I don't know, man. I don't know you anymore. I don't know me. I don't know."

"He's here. Last chance to see your dad. It's either me or you that goes. He said he needed two of us. Then he'd bring him back for real. What would you do? If you could get your dad back, man, what would you give?!"

"I wouldn't give you, Pilar. I wouldn't give Bobby."

Pilar began to cry. I could hear him. He dropped the bat; it clattered on the walkway. The rope hit the patch of dirt in the grass we used for home plate.

"I love you," I swore I heard him say. He didn't scream like Bobby but his anguished gasp revealed the pain. When noise returned to the world, and I could overcome my fear enough to move, I opened the door.

Pilar had brought more than a rope and a bat. In his school backpack, by the curb, I found a carving knife, handcuffs (in case the rope didn't suffice, I guess), a barbecue lighter, lighter fluid, and - the coup de gras - a letter written by Pilar. In it, he explained how all three of us had run away.

I sat on the curb with that letter in my hands till about midmorning. My mom came out and found me. Police were called but I couldn't speak much about what had happened.

Pilar's written version became the dominant narrative. They figured, I think, that I had chickened out on taking off with my friends. Offering a fragmented tale about our dads coming back (but actually not) made me look crazy.

I went home. I fell asleep.

That's when I woke up at 2:59 AM again.

He spoke softly but clear. "Son, it's me. It's okay. You can come out now. Son, come on down."

I didn't go. I don't think I breathed.

It stopped. I didn't wake up at that time. Not for the longest time.

Life resumed. Kind of.

Nothing good about Ferry Street remained for my mom or me. We moved across town, and carried on the best we could.

I did all the things I was told to do but didn't make any lasting connections. The hollow feeling never went away. Once in a while, I could forget about those nights. I could pretend to be someone else in a crowd.

But real joy has never been mine. Days and moments usually associated with happiness are reminders of what I've lost. To say my sanity is compromised regularly would be accurate.

I wouldn't have written anything about this but then it happened again.

I woke up at 2:59 AM.

I didn't get out of bed.

But it hasn't stopped.

I wake up at the same time every night, and have for the past two weeks.

And last night, I didn't go to the window.

I went to the door. I grasped the handle and couldn't think of one reason not to go outside.

Only soul rending fear kept me in. Keeps me in.

But I could overcome it. Pilar did.

Maybe tonight.

If I open it, I'll see his face again, one more time, alive, and then it'll finally be over.

Dolls Don't Eat

THE DISPATCHER SAID two kids - boy and a girl - showed up on a lady's doorstep. Lady said the kids wouldn't talk or give their names. She gave them milk and cookies and sent them to rest in her bed because they looked tired.

No children had been reported missing but it was late, so the dispatcher thought the parents didn't know their kids were gone.

No problem. Not my first call about kids that walked out the front door because they wanted to play. At least it wasn't winter.

I drove to the house on the outskirts of Bridal Veil Lake. It looked like another farm sold off for condos that were never built. A bunch of wild fields and dirt surrounded the lady's house. It was remote and dark and I wondered if she felt comfortable living alone out here.

That knock in the middle of the night must have been a shock.

I announced my presence and knocked lightly. "Hello?"

An old woman - the lady - answered. "Hello," she said.

"Hello," I said again. "How are you doing tonight, ma'am?"

"Been better. They're in the bedroom. Sleeping, I think." She stepped aside to let me in. I saw two shapes beneath a quilt in the darkened bedroom.

"There was no one else? You didn't see anybody?"

She shook her head.

"Were they injured? Scared?"

"No, just shy. Really shy." She nodded toward the kitchen, which I could see from where I stood (not a big house). "They hardly ate."

There were two neat piles of chocolate chip cookies beside full cups of milk. It all looked completely untouched. The sight made me antsy.

She said they didn't eat much. They ate something then but not a crumb had fallen on the table? Nuh uh. I have three kids. Never saw them leave a cookie intact or at all.

Something really bad must have happened with these children.

"Hi kids," I said quietly from the doorway of the bedroom. I didn't want to startle them. "Are you awake?" No answer. But I had to check on them.

There was only a lamp for the room, and it barely lit anything. Two small shapes lay with their whole bodies and heads covered with the quilt, completely still.

"I'm a policeman," I said. "I'm here to help you. You don't have to be scared."

I waited. Still nothing.

"I'm going to pull off the blanket very slowly, just so you can see me, okay? Then you can put it right back, if that makes you feel safe."

Nothing. They didn't move a muscle. I prepared for the worst, and pulled off the quilt.

Their eyes were black, shiny, and lifeless.

"Jesus..."

Because these were not living children but life-sized dolls... complete with clothing and realistic hair. Only the eyes in their plastic faces looked immediately fake.

"What the hell..." I stomped out, admittedly pissed off. The lady waited in her living room chair. "Is this a joke?"

"Excuse me?"

"Those aren't real kids," I said, "they're dolls."

She became confused. "I beg your pardon?"

I took a breath, and tried to calm down. "Ma'am, are you on any medication or..."

She got up and went to the bedroom. "Jesus Christ, save us..."

I shouldn't have let her see. The lady fainted at the foot of the bed. I called it in, and everyone had a good laugh about the dolls - except me.

The lady had been prescribed blood thinners and a nasal spray for seasonal allergies. Unless she did other, non-prescribed drugs, she had nothing hallucinogenic in her system. That meant she probably had a tumour or dementia. A gas leak could also be a possibility.

I mulled over these details while I escorted the ambulance to the hospital. She wasn't unconscious for long but didn't fight my suggestion to see a doctor.

"Thank you," she said from a stretcher, squeezing my hand, just before the paramedics wheeled her into the ER. I nodded. I didn't know what to say. It's my job to help.

I followed them in. Sometimes doctors want to ask us questions. The cafeteria called to me. Four more hours till the end of my shift. Coffee and a sandwich seemed prudent. I hardly touched them.

The walkie crackled. There'd been an assault at the hospital. Obviously, I responded.

"Someone's been attacked," dispatch said. "The nurse that called wasn't very clear, and she hung up."

I got up from the table the same time a doctor descended the steps into the food court and shouted something incomprehensible. When he got close, I grabbed him by the shoulders.

"She's dead," the doctor said. "Gone. He killed her!"

It took a bit to understand. I'll summarize: the old lady I'd escorted to the hospital had been murdered by another patient, a young man suffering from unmedicated schizophrenia. He'd been brought into the ER after being hit by a car.

"I thought he was sleeping," the doc had told me. He sat on the floor with his head in his hands. "Oh god, her head. He cut off her head."

Apparently, he walked down the hallway with it. Then he sat down and chatted with staff until the police arrived. I never left the food court, so I was spared the scene.

Still messed me up. She thanked me. I'd sent her to her grisly death.

A tragedy. That's what everyone, including my therapist, said, and I eventually agreed. I believed it.

For years, I didn't think about those dolls unless someone brought them up. The old woman had been suffering from some kind of delusion. No point in finding out what exactly with her gone. Probably wouldn't even be possible.

Then I got another call.

"What? What did you just say?"

This dispatcher didn't know about the kids and the dolls. That was half a decade ago by this point. "Can you hear me?"

"Yes."

"North side. A gentleman says two kids showed up on his doorstep. No missing children reported tonight."

"A girl and a boy? The kids?" I asked.

"Yeah, how did you know?"

I didn't explain. "I'm on it but send more constables please."

So many similarities to the previous tragedy: the time of year, the wrong side of midnight, and the kids gaining entry to the home.

Except that hadn't happened last time. They were dolls, I reminded myself. I would go to the house - in the posh side of town - and find actual kids there. Then I would do my job and get them home.

Fear against resolve, I gripped the steering wheel too tight and my fingers went numb. Big dead hotdog fingers trembled when I got out of the cruiser in the huge driveway.

No lights were on in the mansion at the top of the hill. I'd hoped the other constables would have arrived but I was alone again. Took me a few moments to calm down and not call dispatch for an ETA.

As I approached, I could see the front door had been left slightly open. My flashlight revealed a foyer big enough to fit a house. Since there hadn't been a crime reported, I felt confident to call out to the owner.

"Hello?" An echo replied. The place really was that big. "Bridal Veil Lake PD. Your front door is open sir." I rang the doorbell and waited a bit. Nobody showed.

I don't know why I didn't call dispatch or wait for the other constables. The only reason I went in, I think, was because I had to know if history was repeating. "I'm coming in."

The switches were dead. No power.

Grand staircases wrapped the foyer in a broad embrace and in the center, they were there, propped up before a headless storyteller. At first, I didn't understand and I tried talking.

"It's going to be okay," I said, to a headless man. He'd been posed with an oversized Grimm's fairytale book between his thigh and arm.

Before each of the black-eyed dolls, set up to appear as attentive children, a tall glass of milk and a bowl of chips had been placed and left untouched.

I choked out a gasp. It couldn't be. It couldn't. How could the dolls be here?! Attempts to draw my firearm and use my radio went about as well as you can imagine. The gun hit the marble floor and I communicated nothing of use to dispatch.

Maybe that was good. I might have shot the other constables when they showed up. They found me on my knees and hysterical. I kept pointing at the dolls. They thought I meant the headless victim.

"It's going to be okay," one of them said, and it felt like I'd said it. Or this constable had been cloned from my cells. Funny the places a shattered mind wanders.

"Okay?" I asked. I don't remember much after that. I went to the hospital. They had to sedate me. I wouldn't stop talking about the dolls.

"Olive and Matthew," my therapist said. He'd come to visit, and explain what had happened. "It's a terrific coincidence," he said. "Those dolls are the same, yes, from the last incident. Apparently, they didn't belong to [the woman who passed]."

I don't know why this information horrified me. "Well who the hell do they belong to?!" I shouted.

"It's alright," he said. "It's not entirely what you think."

He really pissed me off. "Look, just fucking explain it then."

"Right, sorry, okay, the dolls weren't known to the relatives. They claimed [the lady who'd been decapitated] didn't like dolls of any kind. She found them creepy. Your colleagues put them into evidence for lack of a better option. Then they were sold at auction."

"And the rich guy bought them?"

"No," my therapist said. "But somebody did, and that person... Well, they're the killer, I'm afraid. A man was discovered in the mansion basement, covered in blood and with the head."

"I thought you said it'd be alright?!"

"The man was mentally ill," he went on, "but he bought those dolls. Maybe he even called about the kids. Do you see what I'm saying?"

"Some kind of copycat killing?"

He shrugged his bony shoulders in his tweed coat. "It's the only thing that makes sense. Perhaps he knew the other schizophrenic man that killed [the woman who thanked me]. The important thing to note is that nothing supernatural is occurring." The therapist smiled.

"What?"

"It's an unfortunate coincidence, I mean." That bullshit smile twitched. I've been around long enough to know when someone is pulling a con.

"I never thought it was supernatural," I said. "Why did you say that?"

He chuckled nervously. "An unfortunate choice of words. I didn't mean to imply that-"

"How do you know the names?"

"The names?"

"Of the dolls," I said, before attempting to get out of the hospital bed. Handcuffs held my wrists. The sedatives prevented this observation until the urge to punch the therapist moved my body. "What the hell is going on? Why are you telling me this? You're not from the department! What the fuck is happening?!"

He backed away toward the door. "Calm down. The killer named them. He kept saying the names over and over. The inspector contacted me. She thought it best I talk to you. I agreed and-"

"Bullshit."

He suddenly went mute with his lips mouthing the words, "Help me" over and over. His eyes darted to the little window in the door at the same time a shadow passed across his face. The therapist shivered and sniffled back tears. "You should run," he said, his last words.

All at once, the man collapsed.

"What the fuck?! Help! Help!" I shouted.

The nurses came and did their thing but he was gone.

"He's gone?" I asked. They stopped trying to revive him. One of them confirmed it.

How had he died? A real tragedy. Another unfortunate coincidence. The deceased therapist had an unknown aneurysm that just happened to trigger while he begged for help and a shadow crossed the window.

Bullshit.

I took his advice.

After my wife picked me up from the hospital, I told her I would take early retirement. She looked relieved until I told her we needed to leave Bridal Veil Lake.

I purchased a cottage up north on Oxbow Lake. My family didn't come. Who can blame them? I didn't think they were in danger until I learned everybody is and there are no safe places.

They came on the third night.

At first, the knocking struck too softly. I thought I imagined it. Then it became more persistent, more rapid.

I didn't move from the recliner or even lower the footrest. I just watched the door and did my best not to breathe too loudly.

The knocking continued with desperate urgency. Then tiny fingernails scratched at the door. Soft weeping followed that, a child for sure. I could no longer be idle.

I went to the window and peeked through the curtains. The expected pair - Olive and Matthew - wept in the gloom of the stoop.

They weren't dolls. They were kids. Flesh, blood, and human.

I relented and opened the door.

The very images of the dolls looked up to me. Misery and fatigue had captured the innocence from their faces. I know what an overtired child looks like. This wasn't that. The little boy and girl hadn't rested in days.

They swayed on their feet, avoiding collapse by way of fear of something greater. I just didn't know that yet.

I'm not crazy. I don't believe in ghosts or whatever shit this was supposed to be. I hadn't been drinking anything but pop and there were no gas leaks in the cottage or the monoxide detectors would be going off.

The kids were real, and they were scared.

But so was I. I grabbed their arms and basically tossed them behind me and into the living room. It's so dark on Oxbow Lake with a million places to hide.

I shut the door and threw the bolt.

Olive and Matthew clutched one another by the recliner.

"What's going on?" I asked. "Who are you? How did you get here?"

They stared but not at me or anything. Both were underweight and filthy. A combination of urine and stale sweat emanated from their simple clothes.

"Go to the couch," I said, "lie down." Completely aware of the pattern I was fulfilling, I went to the kitchen and grabbed some apples and cheese. I set it down on the coffee table.

"Eat," I said.

Neither would look at the food.

"Eat," I said, louder. They had to eat. It felt crucial. If they ate, then they were real because the food would be gone, and that seemed like tangible proof of their existence.

Olive yawned. Matthew's expression contorted with scorn while his bottom lip trembled. He seemed angry with her. She looked ashamed. Both started to cry again.

"What the hell happened to you?"

I dialed 911, and went through the process of summoning the police. The dispatcher thought I was crazy when I demanded a severe response.

"You'll be lucky to see a constable within an hour, sir," she said. "You're so far away."

I couldn't argue with that but tried anyway. "I'll be dead before that. Something isn't right." I told her about the dolls and my time with BVLP. She listened intently because of her training.

Talking was good. Talking meant life and focus off of whatever she might believe I could be capable of. The call hadn't gone well, in other words. I'd simply cast myself as a crazy, possibly dangerous suspect.

I hung up. Maybe they'd get here fast because of the kids. Maybe I'd be beheaded, long before a hope of rescue.

The kids leaned into the cushions, closed their eyes, and immediately fell asleep. No bites had been taken from the food.

I got my gun from the bedroom.

When I returned, the dolls were beside them. All four could be mistaken for sleeping children. A tall, disheveled man stood by the peeled screen of the open window. Only his fingernails, bitten and jagged, caught the edge of the lamplight.

Shadowed lips muttered gibberish at first but then his word became clear. "Dolls don't eat, dolls don't eat, dolls don't eat..."

I aimed. He lunged. I fired. He staggered but not before wrapping his large hands around the barrel of my gun. I put another bullet through him and yet he didn't fall. With surprising strength, he smacked me across the face.

I dropped the gun.

He retrieved it, and somehow our positions in the living room were reversed. He stood near the couch - the real kids had run away. Only their simulacrums remained. I stood near the expertly sliced screen of the front window.

The man's narrow head resembled a crescent moon. He appeared confused by the blood exiting his body as he struggled to level the gun. I wasn't about to wait around for him to figure it out.

I leapt through the open window as a bullet shattered the glass above my head. My ass hit dirt and I tore off into the pitch of the forest, figuring I'd hide somewhere until the police arrived.

And for a while that worked. I lay in the midst of some thorny brush - scratched me up good - until time enough said that man had to be dead from blood loss. I endured the escape from the brambles, crawling until something firm pressed between my shoulder blades.

"There you are," said a voice, impossibly calm and smooth. "Don't move. I have you. The blade is sharp and I have done this before." I did as he said and remained as still as my fear would allow. "Of course, you understand something about it now?"

When I remained silent, he ordered an answer, punctuating the request with the tip of his knife. "You make them knock on doors in the night. They're supposed to be like dolls? And if they're not..."

"Then the kind caretakers have to die," he finished. "Olive and Matthew must become the same as their dolls. Exactly the same."

"Why?"

The knife point penetrated slightly. "That's not for you to know. We're only here because of bad luck. You happened upon two instances of their training. They were so little that first time. They're older now, but don't look it. We don't let them grow much."

"You cut off that woman's head in the hospital," I accused.

The knife pressure relaxed slightly. "Perhaps I was wrong, and you don't get it."

But then I did, and resumed tension forced me to reveal everything. "You didn't kill that woman. You didn't kill the rich guy. And you weren't going to kill me." The moon face guy had been a ringer for murder just like the other two. Where did he find so many mentally ill people to take the fall?

He'd need access.

He'd have to be a doctor of some kind.

Or a therapist.

"You're alive," I said. "You didn't die in the hospital. No aneurysm. How is that possible? The nurses..."

The therapist laughed. "Elementary, my dear Watson. I made up a story for the nurses. Told them you were dangerous, and obsessed with me. I needed to cut contact with you and, while certainly dramatic, they were all too willing to help out a colleague."

"You wanted me to go far away," I said.

"I hoped you would, but never thought you'd be so dense as to choose yet another perfectly isolated location for me to work. You would have been much safer in your home."

I was too scared to feel stupid.

"Now we're going back in to see Olive and Matthew," he said. "My poor slave is likely dead, so it's my turn to cut, and that's fine. I'm out of practice and there's no need to rush."

"Why let the victims contact the police?"

"The children have to see that no one can help them. They are mine. Makes it more fun too."

"But why the dolls? You're leaving a trail."

He snickered. "Less than breadcrumbs. Only you've connected two of the scenes and I've left dozens over the years. Granted, the last one was dramatic. I couldn't help myself. I wanted Olive and Matthew to see what happens to good people when they disappoint me."

I thought of Olive's yawn and how hungry they must always be. "One of them ate."

The knife pierced my skin and I gasped and writhed.

"Dolls," he seethed, "don't eat. Now get up. Up! Into the house. And-"

The distant thrum of an engine filled the otherwise perfect quiet of the lake. Noise travels easily across water, so he waited and listened. When it became clear a vehicle approached, he drew in a sharp breath and exhaled slowly, calming himself.

"Well, someone's coming. It happens."

"Are you going to kill me?"

The pressure of the knife tip evaporated like the presence of the psychopathic therapist. I leapt to my feet and threw a wild punch in the dark. Nothing but air swept over my knuckles.

"Coward," I said. "I won't keep quiet. I'm not afraid," I lied, badly. "I'll find you. I'll find those kids! You hear that! I'm coming Olive! Matthew!"

He chuckled, already some indeterminate distance away. "Good luck. Tell anyone you think cares or will believe you."

Headlights bounced down the narrow dirt road. The front door of the cottage opened and filled with the therapist. I screamed and rushed him and realized my next mistake too late.

The man wasn't the therapist but an off-duty park warden, keenly aware of his surroundings and the clumsy charge of an old, wounded cop. He flipped me with some kind of judo. I landed across the coffee table, on the untouched food, facing the black eyed dolls.

A pair of cuffs came next. I ranted about the dolls and the therapist and the children to no avail. They found the moon faced martyr crouched by the broken window. Even dead, he still appeared confused.

The warden used his cell to call for more support.

The dispatcher had only called him because she knew he lived near Oxbow Lake.

I told the story so many times, and begged them to look for the therapist and those kids. Hours later, someone must have called him because they came back with another unfavorable fabrication:

The therapist had never left Bridal Veil Lake, and answered the call from Huntsville police on the landline of his office.

"He drove back," I said. Huntsville and Oxbow Lake is roughly five hours away from Bridal Veil Lake. I'd been questioned for six.

"He also told us about your... condition."

I laughed. "Sure, sure, of course. But what about the break in and the dolls?"

The constables looked at one another. "We asked about that. He said it's possible - perhaps even likely given your trauma - that you took those dolls from evidence. That's where they were after your last... discovery. You had access and a reason to dwell on them."

"A reason..." They were choosing their words carefully. "What about the intruder?"

"He's local. An addict. Really ill. He's been arrested for breaking into cottages before. But usually goes for empty ones. You just moved to Oxbow. Even with lights on and a vehicle out front, he probably didn't understand it was occupied. You surprised him."

"I surprised him?" I asked, incredulously.

After many more protests, I was released and told to be grateful. An investigation would follow, of course, but no charges laid unless something more incriminating was found.

"It won't be," I said, bitterly.

The constable walking me out of the Huntsville station just shook his head and walked away. "Man doesn't know how lucky he is."

Before I could object, the doors shut.

I packed my shit and raced home. I didn't have my gun, of course, but figured he wouldn't be armed at his office. If he was, it'd be with that knife. In a fair fight, I'd take it and cut his damn head off.

Ignoring the protests of his secretary and the man seated in his treatment room, I found him.

He appeared alarmed, scared. "Are you... what's the matter?"

"What?" I scoffed, "Didn't expect to see me again?" I moved closer to his desk and he stood up before backing away to the large window. We were on the fifth floor of the building. "Where are they?"

"Who-"

I braced my foot against his desk and pushed it slowly until his legs were trapped against the sill. "Olive. Matthew."

"I don't-" He yelped when I pushed harder. "I swear! The police in Huntsville... they called. I understand something happened up there but I can assure you-"

"You died in the hospital," I seethed. "Right in front of me."

He looked to the other man in the room, his patient. "I didn't visit you in the hospital... I... I'm not dead. You're PTSD must have caused a psychotic break and-"

"Liar!"

We argued more but then the BVLP showed up, and I was strongly encouraged to leave, which I did. I refrained from telling him "this isn't over" because I'd be arrested.

He knew anyway. He counted on it.

I went home next and tried to talk to my wife and family. He'd called them first and told them to be careful and call the police if I began behaving erratically.

My story, of course, fell into that category.

"You can't stay here," my wife said, and it hurt to know she couldn't believe me and never would. I left without argument.

He found me later in the park at night.

The nervous demeanor had been left behind for his patients and the rest of the world. He lit a cigarette and asked if I wanted one.

"You son of a bitch," I said.

He exhaled a plume into the air. "So now you understand?"

"How I'm about to kill you? Sure." I had nothing to lose.

"They're dead if I am," he said, completely calm.

"Seems like I'd be doing them a favour."

He pulled a small pistol from his coat. "No one would be surprised I carried this and shot a crazed attacker."

"What the fuck do you want?" I had nothing left to give him or anyone.

"No one gets away. They have to know."

"So you're going to kill me?"

"Eventually, yes, I will come, and we'll finish what we started. They'll knock in the night and you'll answer the door, let them in, and offer them food."

"Which they won't eat."

He nodded.

"Because they're dolls."

"If they're not by then," he said, "then it'll be over. I'll find others. But I think they'll do fine."

"Tell me why you're doing this. I'm as good as dead anyway."

He held his cigarette in clenched teeth when he smiled. "You'd be shocked how much one will pay for a "doll" of mine. Quite shocked indeed."

"That's not why you do this," I said. Not enough of me remained to shed a tear. I felt hollow, dead already.

I couldn't be shocked anymore. When they knocked, I would open that door. I would try to help them, though it seemed futile, and failure so certain.

He backed away until confident I wouldn't follow. I stayed in the park the rest of the night but moved into the motel where I currently live the next day.

Now I wait.

I typed this all out and put it here, so maybe, when I'm gone - when I'm headless - someone will look for those poor kids and give them something to eat.

This is my last, low hope.

Thank you.

I'm Afraid I'll See My Wife Again

I WISH SHE WOULDN'T do that. I should have told her instead of burying my feelings until they exploded out of my mouth.

"Stop talking to me from another room!" I screamed from the kitchen.

My wife was in the front room, busy at something, probably the fish tank, and attempting to tell me about her day. We'd started the conversation in the kitchen when she characteristically left to do something else in another room.

I used to follow her around but it became apparent she would just keep leaving my vicinity until I gave up the pursuit. Then we'd have a scrambled chat filled with extended pauses and requests to repeat ourselves.

I was annoyed by this quirk of hers. I'm not sure how it didn't drive her nuts. We never really conversed in any ideal or acceptable way.

Bills got missed. Chores left undone. We didn't delegate tasks because our communication habits sucked.

"What?" she called back after my outburst.

"Fucking hellllllllllll!" I roared. "God fucking damn fucking hell! Can you not stay in the same fucking room as me if you want to talk?! You started this fucking conversation!"

For a stretch of too many seconds, there was quiet.

"For fuck's sake, answer me! Or better yet, get in here! Speak to me! To my face! Not from another room! Not from a different floor! Here! Now!" Spittle crawled through my beard like the frothing of a mad dog.

Again, nothing. No response. Fuck this. I scooped up my keys and intended to hit the road for the local pub. When I passed the front room, I hesitated. My wife wasn't there after all.

"Fucking bullshit." It didn't matter where she was, only that she wasn't in the same room as me. I was so pissed, I walked right by the car in the driveway - I usually parked on the street but didn't that day for no reason I can remember - and couldn't be bothered to go back.

As a result, I walked to some basement lounge featuring an awful band and skunky, overpriced beer. After spending too much to get inebriated, I left on the wrong side of midnight but before last call.

The calming effects of the alcohol, and time were a formula for guilt. I felt bad, and intended to apologise to her when I got home, unless she was sleeping.

Lights in the dining room and hallway said she'd waited up.

While fishing for keys, I drunkenly stumbled and shouldered the front door. It drifted open because it hadn't been fully closed.

"Dear?" I called. "Everything okay?"

"Sure is!" she chimed, from the kitchen. The adjacent living room issued the noise of some reality TV show. "Why? What's up?" A girlish giggle bubbled after the questions.

I sighed, already beginning to feel irked. With my shoes still on, I clomped down the hall and into the kitchen. "You left the front-" The lights were off, and so was the TV. She wasn't there.

"Dear?" I thought she might be hiding behind the couch. Maybe she'd felt like drinking too, and believed a lighthearted revenge prank was in order. I probably deserved it, but definitely didn't enjoy the prospect.

I went to the couch and, in the only hiding spot available, there was nothing. The only other place she could have gone would be the back deck, and I would have heard the sliding door open and close. Even drunk, however, I saw the lock had been toggled shut, a feature that only worked from inside the house.

"Dear?" I tried again, figuring I'd simply been mistaken about the TV, and her location.

"Yeah? What's up?" This time her voice and queries seemed to come from the front room. However unlikely, she must have crossed the doorway of the hallway and gone through the dining area without my noticing.

Again, too much alcohol explained the inconsistency.

"Dear, I'm-"

Not in the front room either, but something had changed, evidence of her passing: the light had been switched off.

"Are you running away from me? I understand. I just want-"

"Dear," she called from upstairs, "would you please bring me a glass of wine? The bottle on the counter."

I huffed, but went to do her bidding, though fulfilling such requests always made me feel like a servant. A bottle of cheap merlot, the kind we drank when we were young and broke, waited accusingly by the microwave.

Half had already been drunk, another intentional symbol of what had been lost in our relationship. Pretty passive aggressive, I thought.

"Dear?" she called from our bedroom as I brought the wine. But again, the lights were off. She wasn't there waiting.

"Dear?" I echoed back. "Where are you?"

"What do you mean? I'm over here." She sounded happily confused.

The master bathroom. Light came from under the closed door. The showerhead hissed, and the glass door banged shut. She wanted to drink in the shower, of course.

But when I went in, there again, nothing was as it should be. No bathroom lights. No shower. No wife.

I began to feel uneasy. "Dear? What's going on?"

"Dear?" she called from elsewhere. "The wine?"

"Where are you?" Each time I asked my voice seemed quieter.

"Over here," she said, impatiently.

I went back into the hallway. She'd shut off the lights there too. There were two other bedrooms and another bathroom behind closed doors that always, always stood open before.

"Where-"

"Here!" she shrieked, and it seemed as if her lips grazed my ear. I spun. Some of the wine spilled onto the hardwood. "Over here, dear."

The second bathroom. My hands trembled as I reached for the handle. Light slid from under the door. Another faucet came on. She had no reason to use that tub. We never used it. It was dirty from neglect.

Praying to a god I never believed in didn't help. The bathtub wasn't running. The lights were off. No one inside.

"What the hell is going on?!" I bellowed before shivering, and flinching when she called again.

"Dear?" Her voice became patient again, and seemed to be downstairs. Had she somehow slipped behind my back? The lights had to be a trick. The shower and the tub too. It could only be revenge. Nothing else made sense.

"Stop running!" I shouted. "I'm trying to bring your wine! The wine you asked me to bring!" I tried to laugh but the sound died in my throat as lights from the front hall stretched lazily up the stairs and into the dark hallway where I could hardly dare to move.

"Dear!" she shouted, again close.

"Dear?" Again far, possibly the basement or garage.

"Dearrrrrrrrrrr," once more, like the final breath of the dead.

My nerves snapped and I wobbled forward to the top of the stairs. I had to get out of here. I had wandered into the wrong house, a nightmare. Down, down, down the steps into shadows instead of the light promised a moment ago.

Hands stiff and useless, I tried the door. The deadbolt had been thrown by me. I always locked up everything at night. It stuck a little sometimes. Pulling on the handle and turning the switch required two hands.

Remarkably, I hadn't dropped the wine in my panicked state. Placing the glass on the nearby end table, I ignored another call from her.

"Dear, where are you trying to go? I'm not out there. No one is out there." Her words overlapped one another. No human being talks like that! It cannot be my wife!

I opened the front door to be confronted by an unusually dense fog, full of swirling tendrils reaching forward, coming for me like clawed fingers. All of my short, rapid breaths inhaled the fumes, and smothered my airways. I fell to my knees. My vision began to fade, but not before I saw the legions of tortured visages in the gloom: all seemed to beg for relief until they realised I could do nothing. Their collective anger erupted into a cursed howl. Or maybe they were warning me.

I fell backward into the house before the first foggy finger could reach the threshold. Then I kicked shut the door, and fought unconsciousness until I could cough up whatever plague now lives in the new eternal night outside my home.

I could breathe. I could breathe. That's all that mattered until...

"Dear? What's up?" Cheerful. Too cheerful.

I practically whispered back, "N-nothing, dear." I picked up the wine, and have been trying to bring it to her ever since. It's an endless journey through my house. She does not let me stop. If I try, the calls come sharper, louder, and with promises of harm and death.

"The wine! The wine! I'll have your skin!"

I write on my phone while on the move.

I cannot get out. I am going to die soon, I'm sure. This message is both a plea and a warning.

Help me if you can. Help my wife. I don't know what she has become.

Be kind to your significant other.

You'll miss those pet peeves when they're gone. They are part of the person you love.

I should have been patient. I shouldn't have given up following her. I shouldn't have yelled.

I miss my wife. I'm afraid I won't see her again. I'm afraid I will.

It'll be the end soon if I don't. It will be death, I know, if she lets me find her, if I see the horror I have made.

Thrown To The Dogs

I LOVE MY OLDER BROTHER.

Sometimes, I wish he'd died.

We were kids. I was only ten, and he was sixteen. He had just got his driver's license, and we went everywhere in our town because we'd seen so little of it growing up.

Each night, Jack would make some excuse to take our family k-car - they don't make them anymore - somewhere, and our parents would always go along with it. They knew we were just excited to explore this new freedom my brother had attained.

"Fine, but take Peter with you," my mom would say. I could tell Jack was a bit irritated to have to bring me everywhere. I was his "luggage," as he and his friends had so affectionately defined me. I could have made an excuse not to go, given him space, but I loved my brother.

If he was doing something, then it was worth doing, and I couldn't stand to hear about it secondhand. I wanted to be there, sharing his cool experiences with his group of high school friends. I had no friends my own age. I guess I had no friends.

One such friend of Jack's was Kyle, a goofy, intense guy who could never sit still. He always wanted to pick me up and spin me around. I hated it. Jack made him stop when he noticed my discomfort.

On what turned out to be our last drive around Bridal Veil Lake, we picked up Kyle. He was waiting on the porch in the rain and looked to be in a pissy mood. His discontent worsened when he saw me riding shotgun.

"Jack, really?" Kyle said. "You brought the kid?"

"Get in the back, Pete," Jack said. I crawled between the front seats. I was happy to be there. I didn't care where I sat. Kyle got into the car and slammed the door behind him.

"Drive," he snapped.

"What's your problem?" Jack asked as he backed out of the driveway.

"Nothing," Kyle said. Didn't seem like nothing. "Parents are being jerks again." I didn't understand then that Kyle's parents were alcoholics and nasty drunks, and his homelife made ours look perfect by comparison.

"Sucks, dude," Jack said. "You want to stay at our place tonight?"

Kyle didn't answer. He stared out the window. "It's that way."

"The nunnery?"

"No, the 7-11," Kyle snapped. "Yes, the f-cking nunnery. Where else?"

"You better cool it with the attitude," Jack told him. "Or you can walk."

What could Kyle say to that? Jack could kick him out anywhere, and then he'd have a sad walk back home in the rain. I liked that idea.

We drove for a while in silence until Kyle apologized. "Sorry man, this was supposed to be fun."

"It's no biggie," Jack said. Our dad would say that too whenever we messed up.

"We're going to the nuns?" I asked as the Reliant K-Car crossed the intersection of Ferry Street, where our old house used to be. Neither of them answered my question.

The neighborhood, as most know, has the special privilege of being located a few blocks from a psychiatric hospital and a closed down nunnery. The two institutions used to be associated with the other. Nuns were also nurses during the Korean War, treating veterans with PTSD.

The nunnery had been vacated abruptly in the 1970s, way before I was born, and while the Catholic Church still owned the land, they (the pope?) seemed to forget about it.

Castle-like walls on the grounds were torn apart by strands of strangling ivy. Trees that had been cared for became imbalanced and toppled before slowly dying in the mud. The big house (the convent?) where all the nuns used to live lost its white paint to the elements, and a big crucifix had been dragged from somewhere inside and thrown into the dried out fountain.

This was what I remembered of the nunnery before we moved. When we pulled onto the shoulder by the gate, the crucifix hadn't moved in the intervening years.

"Right where I left it," Kyle said to himself.

I'm not sure if he meant the crucifix or something else. Maybe I didn't hear him right. The rain had intensified and created a racket on the windshield and roof.

"I didn't bring my umbrella," Jack said.

"I'll buy you a whole raincoat after," Kyle said.

"And you're sure it's not stealing?" Jack asked.

"How the hell is it stealing if nobody owns it?"

Kyle had apparently already visited the nunnery a few times to pillage items left behind. He'd sold a rug and some silverware to the pawn shop and made a few bucks.

But he wasn't the only one with the same idea. On his second expedition, he'd heard some movements on the second floor and got freaked out enough to run. Any intelligent person would give up at that point and get a job. Kyle thought it better to rope Jack into the scheme.

Jack was big, tough, and calmly fierce if the situation called for violence. I'd seen him take down the DeRollo twins during an argument over baseball. They attacked him. So it wasn't wrong that he'd defended himself with a baseball bat, and the twins ended up in the ER.

"There's bound to be some good stuff in the basement," Kyle said. "And the rain's letting up. Let's go."

Jack turned to the backseat. "You should stay here, Pete. This won't take long."

"What? No way!"

"I'll lock the doors," Jack pleaded. "Lie down here. No one will see you."

I shook my head. "Jack, no, I can't. Someone will get me."

Kyle chuckled until Jack shut his mouth with a glare.

"Okay, stay close and be quiet."

It felt like a dream. Wet gravel crunched under my sneakers. I stepped in a deep puddle because I stared up at the dark windows, wondering if anyone or anything stared back.

"Jack," I said, "I'm scared. I don't want to go in."

He didn't seem to hear me. Kyle opened the door slowly and turned on his flashlight. The end of the beam showed an empty hallway and a set of stairs leading to the second floor.

Kyle went inside.

Jack guided me forward and knelt down to say, "Stay in front of me, where I can see you, okay? I'm sorry for bringing you here. I know it seems spooky, but it's just an old building. If there's anyone here, they're homeless, trying to stay warm and dry. They won't bother us." He turned on his flashlight and handed it to me.

I felt a little better after his pep talk. It was dark and smelled like a church mixed with dirt, but that was all. Or so it seemed.

In his usual impatient, agitated way, Kyle went ahead, making a ruckus as he opened drawers in an adjacent kitchen and swearing when he found nothing of value. He appeared in the hallway and grasped a doorknob sticking out of the wall I had failed to notice.

"This is the basement," he said, "but it's locked." As soon as he said "locked, " the practically seamless door swung open, which was cause for more swearing. Kyle had been counting on the lock because he thought it meant the basement and its imagined loot were untouched.

"No point now," Jack said. He laid a hand on my shoulder and started turning me around.

"Whoa, wait," Kyle said. "Can we at least look?"

Jack hesitated, and I remember distinctly how he gripped my shoulders and crouched slightly to look me in the eye. "What do you think, Pete?"

I thought we never should have come here. What I said, however, was that we should look. I didn't want to be "luggage" anymore. Jack giving me the power to choose felt like an opportunity.

"Yes, nice," Kyle said. He gave me a high five and rustled my hair. "This kid's getting cool."

It was the nicest thing he ever said to me.

Jack smirked. "He's always been cool. You're just slow."

The chuckle from Kyle was forced. He looked momentarily stung by the barb. I think it was then I began to realize how important my brother's approval was to Kyle.

"Come on," Jack said. "We're wasting time."

I opened the door. The nervous energy returned to Kyle. He was like a dog excited for a walk. My flashlight illuminated rough stone steps, worn smooth with the passage of a thousand feet. The walls were similar, though rougher, and there were hooks supporting oil lamps because no electricity had been extended to this part of the building.

"Creepy," I said.

"Yup," Jack agreed.

"Come on." Kyle took the lead again, and we descended the cylindrical shaft to a shockingly wide and long corridor. The arches in the ceiling, the floors, the walls were all constructed with red bricks shedding their mortar. Someday, the weight of the house above would crush this tunnel. I hoped it wasn't today.

"What is this place?" Jack asked.

Kyle shrugged.

"It's like a dungeon," I said, "look at the -"

The tiny barred window on one of six identical doors I'd been pointing at changed. There'd been some movement there like dirty fingers retracting into a cell.

"What is it?" my brother asked me.

I continued to shine the light on the tiny window, but the sound of a shuffling footstep further along the corridor snatched my attention.

"Did you hear that?" I asked.

"Hear what?"

"Nope," Kyle added quickly. He didn't look scared or was working hard to seem like it. There were three cell doors, evenly divided on the sides of the corridors. At the furthest end there stood a heavier door, blockaded with boards nailed to the frame.

"It's a passage to the hospital," Jack concluded. "The nuns must have done some work here." He didn't add that the work in question was funerary. I found that out later and far too late. Not that knowing in this moment would have changed the outcome.

Like the idiot he was, Kyle went to the big door at the end and tried to pry a board away.

"What are you doing?" Jack asked him. "That probably leads to the hospital."

"Right," Kyle said. The board popped off. Soaked and termite infested wood crumbled in his hands. "So it isn't in use anymore. Maybe it was used for storage for a while."

He didn't say if he meant the nuns or the current hospital staff across the street. Taking things from them would certainly be stealing.

And Jack wasn't interested. "Hey, Kyle, man, we're not stealing from the hospital."

"Of course not," Kyle said too slowly for my liking. "I meant the nuns. Maybe the nuns left something."

"Why would anyone leave something valuable behind a nailed up door?" I asked.

"Ever hear of buried treasure, Pete?" Kyle snapped. "Besides, like you said, we should look. Come on, it's fun."

It was gross and dirty. I didn't move and continued to look at the cells flanking our position in the corridor. There were piles of rubbish underneath a moldy workbench near the bottom of the steps. I encouraged us to search there first, but they were too committed to tearing off the planks.

That's when I heard the murmurs of a prayer.

"Guys," I said. But they were focused on the door.

The voice continued in frantic whispers. "Please... beg you... Michael... do not abandon..."

I thought someone was in one of the cells and that they might be afraid of us. If I were homeless, I'd probably stay in an abandoned place and be afraid all the time about somebody wanting to hurt me too.

"It's okay," I said, still unsure where the scared voice came from. "We're not out to hurt anybody."

Kyle pulled the last plank off the door around that moment.

"Guys," I tried again, but they were talking about what to do next. The door still wouldn't open. Kyle wanted to kick it down. Jack thought they should think about it first.

"...here... come here..." another voice said quietly, and this time I knew which cell it came from.

"Hello?"

"...I'm in here..." It sounded like a man whispering. "Help me. I'm here. Come."

"Guys," I said loudly, and unfortunately, at the same time Kyle started laying the boot to the passageway door. I moved closer to Jack. We exchanged a look. He was sweaty and afraid.

"There's somebody in a cell," I said to him.

He didn't understand. "What?"

Kyle's foot plunged through the rotten door. Immediately, a current of smelly air was freed to caress our faces, our bodies.

"There's somebody -"

Jack reached for Kyle too late. His dumb friend rammed his body into the remnants of the door, and instead of stopping him, Jack tripped and fell on top of Kyle. That is why I was the only one to see.

Ahead, a gently curving ramp ascended, and against a painted wall came the shadow of what I can only describe as a king. His silhouette wore a tall and ornately evil crown, and he laughed as the shadows of several, leashed dogs tugged him down the ramp.

The shadows, however, were all that appeared. Nobody came down that ramp. Only the laughter and the heavy breathing of the dogs continued.

Jack scrambled backward off his friend, and Kyle crawled out of the tunnel doorway. There was nothing to be seen there. Yet, I knew. They did too despite their eventual denials. Something evil lurked ahead, and it had seen us.

Leashes slapped the floor as if dropped and padded feet and claws scrambled for purchase on the smooth concrete. The dogs had been let go. It sounded like it; the tunnel still appeared empty.

"Run!" a female voice shouted from one of the cells. "Run! Runnnnnnn!!!" Her screams rang in my ears.

I don't know who ran first or how I ended up at the door at the top of the basement stairs. When my hands couldn't turn the knob, my legs gave up. The invisible horror pursued us.

Jack raged against the basement exit. Strong arms wrapped around my waist and lifted me and turned. Kyle was screaming in my ear.

"Jack!" I called.

He turned around and saw that Kyle had picked me up as a human shield.

"Jack," I pleaded.

He just watched as Kyle threw me at the growls climbing the stairs. I hit the landing and felt their teeth sink into my flesh. The animals tore away skin and feasted on muscle. I was still alive when they pierced my stomach. When would I die? The pain made me wish for death.

Terrored screams from below, from the cells, suddenly faded. The ordeal was ending. Only one pained howl remained: Mine.

"Pete, Peter, Pete," Jack said over and over.

The basement doorway was open now, and Kyle walked through it. Jack picked up whatever was left of me and placed what had to be a mangled corpse in the backseat.

"Dad," I said, "will be mad about the blood."

Confusion entered Jack's concern. "What blood, Pete? There's no blood. You're fine."

He went to the driver's seat and started the car. Kyle wouldn't look at us.

"Sorry," he said before exiting the car at his house. "Sorry, Pete. I'm sorry you fell. I tried to catch you." It was a lie. I didn't have the will to deny it.

By the time we got home, I realized there really wasn't any blood and no physical injuries at all. I got out of the car and followed Jack inside. Our parents watched TV in the living room while we ate neapolitan ice cream in the kitchen. It seemed very normal until Jack put me in bed and stretched out in his. We shared a room.

"You okay, Pete?"

"Yeah," I lied. "But what happened there?"

He stared at the ceiling. "I don't know."

That was the last we spoke of the nunnery. Jack stopped driving for fun. I stopped hanging out with him. I didn't see Kyle again until a decade later; I was waiting for an order at a burger place, and a completely hairless man walked in. I didn't recognize him as Kyle until I was on my way home. I don't know why he lost all his hair. I don't care.

My brother and I grew apart fast. He hadn't tried to stop Kyle. None of us should have broken into the nunnery.

I never forgot the feeling of being torn apart by dogs. I'd only seen their shadows cast on the wall of the tunnel in waking life. In my nightmares, they were huge mutts with bloodied maws.

The Dark King remained a shadow in both worlds, revealing nothing more of himself but cruel laughter on the wrong side of midnight. I try so hard to sleep, but it's not much better to meet him in the dream. It might be worse.

Jack had been in university a few years by the time I reached high school and gained access to drugs and alcohol. While his life took off into career and family and prosperity, mine declined. I never finished high school, became addicted, and struggled to make a connection with anyone.

Eventually, my parents and Jack ceased contact altogether. I am alone but never enough. His shadow follows. Sometimes, I can smell his dogs. Nothing short of total substance based annihilation of my mind provides temporary reprieve.

I tried therapy, but the experts call my experience a delusion and put me on strong antipsychotic meds that don't help. I went to a priest, but he kicked me out and said I should see a doctor. Rehab didn't work, obviously.

So I'm writing to you.

Maybe you can help.

At least, you care enough to have read this far.

The nunnery isn't hard to find.

I think I have to go back. Most of whatever I am is still there. The dogs want the rest. The king is indifferent, so long as I suffer. I'm tired. There's comfort in giving in and giving up.

I'll be waiting in one of the cells with the others. They know. They'll understand. I hate you, Jack. I miss my brother.

The Chicken In My Teeth

WAKE UP AT 5 AM.

Feed the cats.

Make today's coffee.

Fifty push-ups. Fifty squats. Stretch.

Coffee's ready. Drink a giant cup of black and review emails sent by nervous investors and even more anxiety ridden business partners.

Fifty-push ups. Fifty squats. Stretch.

Ten minutes to expel excrement and respond to important emails, fires that must be put out.

Run on the treadmill for thirty minutes.

Shower.

See wife and children for ten minutes while she struggles to wake them and prepare lunches for school.

Leave for work.

The chicken is in my teeth. It's been there for a few nights already, maybe longer. I don't remember when we had chicken. The piece is stuck between molars on the left side. I work at it with my tongue to no avail during the commute.

Arrive at the parking lot of my business. No, I can't tell you which one. We were new and reliant on some flaky investors. If they found out about the chicken in my teeth, I'd be finished. The business, my dream, would end.

Intend to immediately find some floss in the office. I have a toothbrush in my desk drawer but haven't managed to get the chicken out with it. I need floss or a good toothpick.

Enter the office foyer. Be assailed by the receptionist sheepishly dancing around a request for a sick day.

Grant the request. Move on to the next room, run into business partner with his arms crossed, and a very dark look.

Tell him, "You haven't slept again, Jim."

Listen to the many reasons why he couldn't. Note inwardly they are the same reasons from yesterday and many days before that.

Lie to him. "Everything is going to be fine." Is it a lie if I don't know it to be true? If I feel like it probably won't be fine?

Ignore his tears. Keep moving deeper into the nest of cubicles. Avoid the worried gazes and pretend there aren't several computer monitors displaying job searches.

Enter the corner office. Lock the door. Stare out the window. Nice view of the lake. Wonder if I could swim to the United States on the other side.

The chicken is in my teeth.

Search the desk. There's a plastic sword toothpick from the celebratory drinks handed out on opening day. Go to the mirror on the back of the office door.

Poke the chicken piece with the sword.

"Ouch," it says.

Drop the toothpick. Do not retrieve it. Look at the chicken in my cavernous mouth.

"Ouch?" Wonder if I said it. Think that I didn't.

"Don't poke me," the chicken says, though it has no mouth or head. It is a shred of meat wedged tightly between molars.

Stare in the mirror. What the hell is happening? Begin to sweat. Stress.

"Calm down," the chicken says. Its tiny shred bits vibrate when it speaks, which tickles the tip of my tongue. "Don't do that."

Roll my tongue to the other side of my mouth. Mumble an apology. "Sawee."

"No problem. Listen." The chicken vibrates. "I'm an apotropaic chicken piece."

"A what?" Sound like I'm talking to a dentist with my mouth hanging open while sharp tools scrape and poke.

"I ward off harm that might befall you."

Think about its claim. "Uh huh."

"I'm also alive."

"How are you alive?"

"How are you alive?"

A fair question. Admit, "I don't know."

"Your company is in trouble."

Agree.

"I can help, but you have to follow my instructions no matter how strange they might seem."

Stay quiet. Listen. But agree to nothing. Remember, there is a tiny plastic skewer sword on the floor. I should end the life of the chicken in my teeth because this is insanity.

"Don't," it says. "I want to live. Yes, I can hear your thoughts. Put the sword down and hear me out. You have to go into the kitchen and find a paper bag lunch in the fridge. It'll say Jim on it. Put the lunch in the microwave for ten minutes."

Jim is my friend. He started this business with me. We've known one another since university.

The chicken in my teeth doesn't respond.

"Why should I do this to his lunch?"

"Because it will save the company. It will change everything." The chicken in my teeth has the voice of a soothing doctor. It is the voice of reason and empathy.

Realize there's no other choice. The fledgling dream of a business is on the verge of collapse. Listen to the chicken in my teeth.

March to the lunch room. Avoid gazes and conversation and the stream of concerns.

No one in the lunchroom. It's early morning. Open the fridge. Remove Jim's lunch. Note the heavy weight. Put the bag in the microwave.

Tap the flat buttons. Beep. Beep. Beep. Start for ten minutes of heating. Watch the bag spin in the dull interior of the microwave. Bag catches on fire. More than food there.

A pop. Tiny hole shatters the glass. Feel pain in a rib and a burning sensation. Watch blood soak through my dress shirt. Confusion strangling reason. How could this happen?

Put pressure on the wound. Note the staff crowding by the doorway.

"What was that?"

"Are you okay?"

"Oh my god, you're bleeding."

Chicken in my teeth, why have you forsaken me?"

"Wait," it whispers quietly.

Sit on the floor. Back to the counter, let Farah look at the wound.

"It's not bad." Is she a doctor? A nurse? "Hit your rib."

What hit my rib?

Greg, the college kid, looks in the microwave. "There's a gun in the microwave."

They look at me.

Tell them, "Jim's lunch."

Jim is among them. Notice his guilt, his anger, and confusion. "Why did you do that?"

Ask, "Why did you bring a gun to work, Jim?"

Look at him. Everyone looks at him. Wait for an answer.

Jim calmly explains, "He needs to die. There's a new partner with a lot of money and experience. The partner agreement we signed does not contain the typical spousal clause. His shares would go to me. I will sell them to the new partner at an agreed upon high price that will drive speculation and raise the price of shares. You own shares. You got more shares than pay at this point. If he dies, you'll be rich instead of scraping by, looking for a new job. He has to die."

Watch my co-workers, my friends, exchange looks, considering Jim's proposal. We signed that agreement before we were married, before we had kids.

"Your turn," the chicken says. "Tell them."

Tell them what?

"What you're thinking."

I can't.

"It's your only chance. Trust me."

Clear my throat. Struggle to my feet. Use the counter to help. The microwave is behind me.

Defend myself: "What if Jim, the madman who brought a gun to work, willing to kill anyone for money, dies? Hm? What will happen then?"

"Good," the chicken in my teeth encourages.

Go on. "Who is this new person willing to step in? I'm guessing they don't care which one of us dies. Probably hope you do because you're willing to murder someone."

"But you're suggesting the same thing," Jim says.

Shake my head. "No. This wouldn't be murder. It'd be self-defense. Some feelings about retribution and justice, too."

Room begins to rally to my side. Not physically. It's not a big room. But they're all looking at Jim.

Gently reach through the shattered glass behind me.

"You always were a fucking weirdo," Jim says. "So driven, so disciplined." He mocks me. "Well this time I'm one step ahead." Out comes the other gun he brought to work.

Everybody ducks.

Don't duck.

Bring out the glock in the microwave. It's still a little hot. Fire a gun for the first time. The bullet rips through his left eye.

Jim is dead faster than the present tense.

Screams from co-workers. Pass out. Awaken in a hospital bed. There's an old man with too little skin wrapped around his skull. Like a latex mask dusted with dirt. He sits in a chair, watching me.

"This is the investor," the chicken in my teeth says. "Listen to him."

Chicken! What happened?

"You were overwhelmed by what you've done, and feinted. Not surprising due to the superficial bullet wound and blood loss."

Jim is dead.

"Yes."

Begin to weep.

"I understand your sorrow," the old man says. He is wearing a dark suit and hat as if on his way to or from a funeral. "You killed your friend."

Point out the obvious. "You sent him to kill me."

"Sh, listen," says the chicken.

"No," the man corrects, "we sent the chicken. We are the perfect ones."

Watch as he slowly opens his coat and shirt to reveal a gaping wound, a rotted hollow where his heart should be. Instead, there are maggots and flies attending them. He grins and presents the new contract.

Sign away Jim's shares to the Perfect Ones.

"The chicken must stay in your teeth," he says. "It's the only way this will work."

"I am apotropaic," the chicken reminds.

"That's right," the perfect one says. "Evil against evil." He wheezes because that is how he laughs. The bloodless cavity is hidden again before he leaves.

Take a few days off. Receive bank alerts concerning deposits from companies I don't recognize. Watch the stock respond very favorably to my business.

Know that I am rich by the following week. Celebrate with my wife and children. She quits her job.

Smell the rotting chicken in my teeth. Consider removing it.

"Don't," it warns.

"But I'm going to get sick if you stay. I'm surprised I'm not already."

"I'm all that stands between you and the others you've opened yourself too. Trust me."

Trust it. Fall terribly ill. Tell no one about the chicken. Feel it decay and wither and remain. Refuse wife's recommendation to go to the hospital. Lose track of time, the days, the months. Wake up in the hospital again.

Try and fail to speak. Try and fail to feel the chicken with my tongue. Try and fail to feel my tongue with my fingers. It is gone. Most of my face is gone. Listen as a doctor explains how they had to remove my severely infected jaw.

Why have you done this? I can't feel the chicken in my teeth with my finger. Are you gone?

"I am here," it soothes. "Alas, I have slipped from your teeth and you have swallowed me. I will stay within you until the time has come."

What time? What time?!

Sign the divorce papers. Can't look at my kids being scared of looking at me. Move into the penthouse of a hotel overlooking the lake. Beg for relief from the chicken in my body.

"I can give it to you," it says, "but you must do as I say."

Agree.

"Draw a circle on the wall. Use ashes from the fireplace. Blot everything but a circle in the middle. Think of the name I give you. Don't you dare ever write it. Pray to that name. Give yourself to it."

Do it. It's done. It takes all night. Now I'm gone. I am gone.

Get my body back for minutes a day. A prisoner allowed time in the yard. Wake up in places but never know how I get there.

Run at first. Realize it's pointless.

AP CLERIOT

Time is so brief.
Tell my story.
Rot.
Help.
Dying.
Chicken in my body wants me to die.

Swipe Right To Fight

WHEN YOUR CHILDREN reach a certain age, they attend birthday parties.

You must attend them too.

The party is not for you or any of the other adults standing around. There are attempts at conversation but none are productive. Nobody has time to watch TV or sports and, even if they did, nobody has enough energy to want to talk about such trivialities. Our children are five, and we are their prisoners.

We love them. Yes, we do. We love them so much. We give them every ounce of ourselves and drown in guilt when we inevitably fail at playing the perfect parent.

We even feel bad as the children scream and wreck the house and whine and laugh and cry, and we're sure this waiting room we have made is an inner circle of hell.

The phones come out. We maintain a respectful distance from one another to doom scroll in semi-privacy.

I sit against a wall beside a dust bunny wearing fishy-cracker crumbs in its hair. Just like my house but cleaner. I've a whole herd of dust critters, full of worse things than crumbs: grape halves and bits of cheese mostly.

Obviously, we parents want the birthday party to end, though we can't say why. The next place will also have obligations and duty, and we'll pack all the guilt we brought with us today.

It makes me angry. I'm a good man, a decent father. I provide for my family. I exercise before they wake up so that I'm strong enough to enthusiastically interact with them. No sitting down with the comforting dust that asks for nothing when I am the focus of my children.

There is no outlet for my feelings. No vocabulary for reasonable complaints is given to men. We come off as immature or childish or entitled if we express dismay. Sympathy, if any is given, is brief.

We are alone soon enough if we go on beating our chests or not. So it's better to not; we can still appear to meet the stoic ideal that kills us a little more each time we fail, and succeed, to live up to it. And if you rolled your eyes at these statements, you are a part of the problem. My problem.

They serve the cake.

The cake is not for us.

We sing happy birthday anyway.

A five-year-old boy blows spittle on the candles and the icing.

Then the parents go back to slouching while an exhausted grandmother passes out slices on Styrofoam plates.

I resume scrolling with my dust bunny. There are always ads in my feeds for dating apps, though I haven't used one in seven years because I married my last match and had this kid. One of them, however, manages to disturb my bitter fugue state.

There's a man punching another man under the word Rumblewish, a clever play on words only S.E. Hinton or Coppola fans and users of Plenty of Fish would understand. Then some animated words appear: Swipe Right To Fight in blood dripping red letters. Tap to install.

I don't tap. I'm sure I didn't. I move my finger along the screen of my phone, intending to scroll away, dog paddling for dopamine.

The Google Play Store opens instead and there's Rumblewish. It's been downloaded a few thousand times, and has a perfect rating score. I installed it without much thought, figuring I was about to play yet another violent video game.

Text appears in white comic sans, single imperatives delivered in beats like splashing blood on a floor:

Anything goes!

Film for cash!

Winner takes all!

Losers don't get up!

No running!

Swipe Right To Fight!

The game loads and what I see is familiar. A circular map of an area occupies the top left of my screen. It's practically identical to the ones found in Grand Theft Auto. However, after a moment, I realize it's a real map of where I am, and I am a blue dot amongst a cluster of red dots - other players. There are four people playing Rumblewish on this street alone. I expand the map and see hundreds more have the app in Bridal Veil Lake.

A translucent feed provides faces and profiles, including cash earnings and win-loss records. Much like another well known dating app, I can open myself to messages from others by swiping right and I can refuse a challenger with a left stroke.

I enlarge the map until the house I'm in is represented by a rectangular blue square seen with a birds-eye view. I'm the blue dot. There's a red dot in this house. I look around at the other sad parents strewn about the living room. Only one, a heavy set guy who never took off his plaid jacket, stares.

I shrug at him like "What?"

He taps the edge of his phone and then points at me. I look at my screen. Someone named bigchoo85 has swiped right on my profile, which I've yet to set up. There's just a gray silhouette where I'm supposed to upload a photo. bigchoo85, however, has an image and it's the heavy plaid guy, of course. He clears his throat to grab my attention, and nods toward the hallway.

He wants me to follow, and I do.

When we're in the hallway, he tugs me by the forearm to the door leading to the attached, double garage. It's strangely intimate, and I feel weird.

"I've never done this before," I tell him when we're standing by a workbench. No cars are parked here. Plenty of space for whatever.

"I know," he comforts me. "But trust me, you're going to like it."

"This app is pretty invasive," I say. "Shouldn't it at least wait until I've swiped to show me a user's location?"

"Look," bigchoo85 says, "You don't have to do anything you don't want to. There's no pressure. In fact, that's not allowed. Swipe left, and we both walk out and that's that, okay?"

I find I am nodding.

He takes off his plaid jacket before crossing his thick arms. It's obvious I'm not as strong as him. I'm mostly a runner. This guy looks like a wrestler.

To go left feels like I'd be letting him down. Now there's an odd thought. Am I so programmed to meet the invisible unknown expectations of a child that I now enter all relationships, even with a stranger, that way? I'm getting angry again, which makes me swipe right on bigchoo85.

"Okay, so now-"

The tip of a screw driver digs a trench above my left eyebrow.

"Damn it," bigchoo85 says. He shrugs at my incredulous look. "What? I missed." He tries again, lunging like a fencer and I just barely get out of the way. There's blood trickling into my left eye.

"You fucker," I say.

"Anything goes," is his reply. He backs up and grabs a hammer off the workbench without looking.

"Is this your house?"

"Yup."

"So-"

"It's my son's fifth birthday," he says. I'm surprised he was hanging out with the miserable visitors. I would have been on my feet the whole time, ensuring I could do no more in the endeavor to hold a perfect party for a daughter that would hardly remember the occasion.

"Are you...judging me?" bigchoo85 asks.

"What? For what? No? No."

With the screwdriver, he gestures to a small camera mounted in the corner. "You see that? It's filming, and when I'm done with you, I'll have a year of my son's post-secondary tuition. Two if you die."

"Die?"

bigchoo85 advances as he smiles and nods. "They pay more for that."

"Two years?" That's at least ten grand or, if it's a good school, much more. I'm pretty sure he's going to try with that hammer first since he picked it up. Sure enough, he telegraphs a ponderous swing that I easily dodge. I drive my heel into the side of his knee. I took karate when I was eight. The sensei said it only takes a few pounds of force to break a knee from the side.

bigchoo85 grunts and attempts a limping retreat whilst swinging the hammer defensively. His breath is through his teeth because he doesn't want to scream and alert the party guests to the rumblewishing happening here.

I'm trembling and suddenly feel like vomiting. He's between me and the door. His knee isn't broken, though, he's not putting his full weight on that leg. His eyebrows bounce up and down like, "Well, well, more than I expected."

This time I notice him drifting back to the tool bench. There's going to be something nasty there for me, something worse. I couldn't allow it. I'd be dead if I did.

Without thinking, I rush him, which sounds cool if you follow it with a jump kick of a hurricane nature or at least a punch, but I flap, I flail.

Real fighting isn't choreographed or cinematic. If it's between two non-experts, it's clumsy and embarrassing. Also, as it is now, it's often ineffective.

bigchoo85 finds the mini-sledge he wants and swings it down against my shoulder. Something shifts or snaps or dislocates and my left arm dangles from its socket as I back away.

"No. Don't," I tell him and the words are a new tone of despair. I am going to die at a child's birthday party. "Help!" I yell but there's sudden noise from inside, a cheer mixed with derisive sighs in a chorus.

"I hired a clown," bigchoo85 says and grins. Some of my blood is on his face. No clown is ever welcomed at a birthday party. The exception, apparently, is when you're about to murder someone in your garage. Only a murderer welcomes a clown. I can't believe this will be my last thought.

bigchoo85 grabs another device from the workbench, one I'm not familiar with, and likely the thing he wanted before I ineffectually flail-charged him. He hits a button and something happens - there's a pop and some kind of discharge of electricity.

The man drops in a stiff pile and twitches slightly. It takes me some time to understand he's used a stun gun of some kind, but the device malfunctioned somehow, and he's stunned himself. bigchoo85 is unconscious, and I have the advantage.

There's a red light on the camera mounted in the corner. Extra money is given to those who win and end the lives of their Rumblewish matches. I pick up a flathead screwdriver from the bench.

I check the app, and there's no money, no reward for victory yet. I'm not sure but I think I have to leave first because he can't follow. There's blood in my eye, and I can hardly see. If I leave, there will be some money. That's the idea. But if I stay and carry out the intention behind picking up the screwdriver, there will be more.

I love my daughter. Yes, I do. Would leaving now be giving everything, my innocence, in service? Would the guilt of murdering a helpless man be less than the remorse of her every future failure? I think not and prepare to plunge the screwdriver through his eyelid and into his brain.

The door leading inside whines as it opens. I hide the screwdriver from the five-year-old in the doorway, a boy, the boy whose birthday it is. I smile at him and wave my fingers at him.

"Happy birthday," I say.

He looks at bigchoo85. "Daddy?"

bigchoo85 responds to his child's voice and stirs, coughing and clearing his throat with rumbling dad sounds. His eyes blink open and widen as if awakening from sleep. I've woken up the same way for the past five years. He sits up and receives his son in his arms.

"What's up, kid?" he asks.

"The clown is scary," his boy says.

bigchoo85 nods and struggles to get up until I help him. He mumbles a "thanks" and staggers back inside. I'm not sure what to do next. I look at the app, and there's money and a congratulatory message from a Rumblewish admin.

I'm 1-0 now, and there's another message suggesting I add details and a photo to my profile to increase matches.

When I move, there's a painful pop in my left shoulder; I've unintentionally resocketed my arm. I go to the bathroom, clean up, and avoid the clown as I find my daughter. Thankfully, the clown motivates her exit, and there's no fight.

We're driving home when she notices I can't stop shivering and looking at her in the rear view mirror.

"Daddy's okay," I lie. "I'm just cold." She offers me the blanket on her lap, and I almost lose it right there. But I can't. To do so would bring her into the sacrifice I have made, so she must never know.

My wife spots the difference in me immediately, too. As a fellow martyr, I can tell her everything. She's not horrified. She is not alarmed. Her eyes light up when she sees the money.

"2,000," she says. "Wow." Using my phone, she links Rumblewish with our PayPal account.

"How does it work?" Her question is eager and more to herself than me. After we put our daughter down for the night, she reads more about Rumblewish and even finds the video of my fight with bigchoo85.

I can't watch it. She does, though, and when I look at her, she cups my cheek and whispers into my ear, "You're a good dad." It's all I've ever wanted. I'm finally able to cry because I know what she'll ask for next, and I know I can't refuse.

• • • •

I'VE BEEN A "GOOD DAD" five more times now. My wife encouraged me to quit my job and work out and take Brazilian jiu jitsu at a local dojo.

I have earned the bonus money twice. I will do it again. For her. For my daughter. To do otherwise would be to invite guilt into an already tortured mind.

Obviously, I can't stop. If something were to happen to the app, however, impeding its function, then this line of income would end.

My wife and I have discussed - and I think I convinced her - there could be more money in a tell-all book or movie deal if Rumblewish becomes known to the world.

We're worried, however, about the people behind the app. They are not good people, obviously, and seem to have money and influence. I think the reason no one has come forward already is because they probably have and then promptly been made to disappear.

There are names of users that say deceased but no record of who killed them in a fight and no footage. I suppose natural causes or a random accident is possible, but I don't know. It doesn't seem likely.

Obviously, I can't help you should you choose to investigate this. If you're interested in becoming a user, however, you can only find the ad and the app if you're already in the vicinity of an existing user. I will be on Tour Hill all next week. Lots of fighters there.

Sincerely, the odd parent meandering everywhere.

What's Inside The Awful Man [NEW]

HE ARRIVED FROM THE darkest part of the closet. That's where I would go when they were done with me. Another evening of pain without reason. I think I was four.

"I can help," he said. It was easy to believe him because he looked like he really could help. He was bigger and scarier than my parents. "I'm not afraid of anything. Or anyone."

When he stood up, I saw how huge he could be, a man marked with foreboding signs on his skin and an empty stare that saw nothing but looked through all, including me.

As a small child, I was used to false promises and lies, so I didn't answer until our meetings had become part of the ritual of abuse.

"That looks painful," he said, referring to a swelling cut above my eye.

"Who are you?" I asked him.

"I've a lot of names. Call me Mike."

"That's like my name," I said, "Michael."

"Is that so?"

I was too young to realize he already knew my name, and that his name was not Mike. He held a palm to my cheek and smiled.

"It doesn't have to be like this," he said.

"It doesn't?"

He shook his bald head. "You'll understand when you're older. For now, go to the freezer and get something frozen. A bag of peas. Wrap it in a cloth and put it on your face, where you hurt. It'll help."

I did as he said, and it did help. I slept in the closet with Mike that night, and most nights after that. Years together drew us closer, and I spent any free time I had with him, though he didn't talk much unless something bad happened or I had a question.

"Why do you never look at me, Mike?" I asked him one morning. I was thirteen.

He frowned as he always does before breaking into a smile and answering. "I always look at you, Michael. This is just what it looks like when one sees everything."

"Everything?"

"Yes."

"Do you know the future?"

"Yes."

"My future?"

"Yes."

"What's going to happen to me, Mike? Am I going to die in this house?" Things had been worse then. They'd stopped buying food. Not that there had ever been much.

Mike looked really sad and turned away to face the wall. He'd never moved from his position in the end of the narrow closet except to stand up and sit back down.

"Yes, Michael," he said. "You will. Unless..."

"Unless?" Despite everything that had happened, I didn't want to die. I wanted to be free. I wanted to live.

"There's a way," he said. The deep voice I'd come to find soothing sent a shiver across my arms. "But it will require great trust. Trust I know you have no reason to give to anyone."

"I trust you," I said truthfully. If the alternative was certain death, what choice did I have?

Mike turned around. His plaid shirt was open and a gigantic mouth unzipped across his large stomach. When it opened, several rows of sharp teeth were revealed.

"Climb in, Michael," he said. "It's the only way."

Staring into the pitch within made my stomach uneasy. "I can't. I'll... be cut to pieces."

"You have to trust me." He ran a thumb over the first row. "They all point inwards, so they won't cut you. It'll be like going down a slide. See?" He presented his unharmed thumb.

"What will happen?"

"I'll protect you. No one will know where you are." Mike smiled and the belly mouth mimicked the expression. "No more evenings with your parents. No more pain, Michael. I'll take it all for you."

"You will?" The tears came so fast it surprised me. No one had ever stuck up for me. No one had put me first. I still didn't understand what Mike really was, but at that moment, he was the person I loved most.

The front door of the apartment swung open and banged the wall. One or both of them were home, and they'd already started.

"Michael!" It was my mom.

"Come in, Michael," he said. "They'll be here soon. No point in enduring it when you don't have to."

One last look at the closet exit, and I swung my feet up. Mike gave me a small push and I went down the surprisingly long slide to the interior where I lost every sense of my body. I could see the world outside the body but not with my eyes exactly. Sight in the traditional sense isn't the right word either.

It's like I could feel and smell and see, and yet not enjoy or indulge or be revolted by any of it. I suppose it was mere awareness through the insulation provided by Mike.

"Michael!" Dad had arrived too. I could hear him and I was afraid. For the first time, Mike left the closet. He went down the hall, letting his fingertips drag over the walls like the rigid claws of a dog.

When they saw him enter the living room, they froze.

"Something the matter?" Mike asked calmly.

"Michael-"

"It's Mike, you bitch." Mike picked up a half empty beer bottle from the coffee table and took a sip.

"The fuck?" Dad was surprised and not pleasantly. He was big and tattooed too and fast. But not faster than Mike. He flipped his grip around the bottle and brought the fat end hard against Dad's face, knocking him flat.

Mom screamed and tried to run, which seemed to excite Mike.

"What's wrong, mom?" Mike mocked her. "I thought you liked watching." He snagged her hair and punched between her shoulder blades, taking the scream right out of her mouth.

From there it became a massacre. He dragged her to Dad and stomped on the side of her neck. She went limp.

Dad saw and his eyes bulged as he realized what Mike had done. "No, wait, pl-"

The shattered beer bottle tore into his eye before he could finish. Dad screamed and begged until he too was dead.

Soaked in blood, Mike went to the kitchen and drank a glass of water before wiping his face with a wet cloth. He picked up Mom's cell and called the police.

"You'll be arrested," I cautioned, uncertain he could hear me from inside.

"Nah," he said, "it was self defense."

I had mixed feelings about my parents' murders. Sure, they deserved to die for what they'd done to me regularly. But the incredible violence made me figuratively sick.

Strangely, Mike could sense the anxiety his actions had produced. "Sh," he soothed, "it's okay. It's over. You're free."

I accepted his comfort and let the numbness at the edge of consciousness take me into rest deeper than sleep. If I could exhale still, I would have. Instead, I took joy in the thought of simply being allowed to live after today.

"Mike," I said, "thank you. When should I come out?"

Sirens entered the range of his hearing. "Wait a bit more. There may be more trials ahead. Rest if you can. You've been through so much."

"Okay. Thank you."

"No worries, kid."

The police arrived with their guns unholstered. They took Mike to the station and were very kind, giving him a sandwich and a coke. He showed them his arms and legs and took off his shirt. I guessed they were interested in all his tattoos.

I'd never really considered them much until then. I was too busy worrying about myself. The tattoos were scary monsters, demons of fire and some of ice. Many others were smaller creatures made of knives and another on his back was made of black leather, and it made me think of Dad's belt, the one he never wore but used every night.

"Why did they do it, Mike?" A surge of emotion came so suddenly that even Mike felt it and had to sit down. He put his big head in his hands and closed his eyes.

"Quiet, Michael," he said, firmly. "I need you to be quiet. If we're going to survive, you must be quiet."

"Okay." I did my best and tried to focus on other things. I was free. They were gone. Nobody would hurt me ever again.

"I'll make sure of that, kid," Mike added. The next week tired him out. So many meetings with doctors and therapists and a judge. Or maybe a lawyer. A huge benefit of living inside Mike was the ability to sink beneath the numbness and just be without thought or opinion. He would take care of it.

For so many years, he did. Some old folks took Mike in because it was their job or something. They were grouchy, at first, but became very careful once they learned what Mike had done to Mom and Dad. He told them they had nothing to worry about so long as they let him be and did what the law required of them.

They did and kept their distance and that was fine for both of us. School went better than it ever had before. Like me, Mike could barely read. Math was easier. Where he thrived, of course, was anything hands on, physical. I watched from within when he started football and dominated the field with ferocity.

Hurting others thrilled him. The violence motivated me to retreat while he played. I liked the end of games, where they patted Mike on the back and invited him to parties. That's where he had his second taste of alcohol.

When he'd had maybe six drinks, he turned inward to me and spoke. It felt like he hadn't in a long time. "It's good, isn't it?" The exit from his body appeared in the void, and the teeth were there but no longer safe. Going down had been a slide. Up would require traversing a field of razors naked. Where my clothes were or how I even knew they were gone, I don't know. I reached for the first row.

"Don't," Mike said. "It'll hurt."

I relented. He allowed the buzz to fill me and I'd never felt better in my life. "It is nice," I assured him. "Can we have some more?"

Mike laughed and the party raged until he got carried away to destruction on a river of alcohol. Other kids clustered on one side of the room and watched as Mike punched through the drywall. It started as a joke. He took it too far and his thick hands bled. The police came and he ran away with the crowd.

Aside from that, however, he did okay and suddenly high school ended. Mike didn't have the grades for college and little money. The old folks couldn't get funding for taking care of him anymore, and rather than tell him to leave, we arrived home one evening to find the locks changed and his few possessions piled on the curb.

He hucked a piece of limestone through the window and proceeded to rob the wisely vacated house.

"Won't you get in trouble?" I asked.

"Need food to survive. Money for a place to stay." He took the old lady's stash of pills and some cash from her disgusting underwear drawer. To further punish them, Mike tossed their nicest clothes into the shower and thought about setting them on fire.

"I don't know, Mike." They weren't the best, these people, but they weren't my parents either. After some hesitation, he turned on the faucet and took us away.

He found a motel on Tour Hill that would accept cash and we stayed there for a week. Mike didn't do much but eat and drink, and, for the first time, I thought about leaving him.

"No," he said before I could ask.

"Why? There's nobody around. If things get scary, I'll come back in. I can't live here forever. It's been years, Mike. I'm eighteen, right?"

"You are," he said. "But the danger isn't over yet. Wait a bit. Wait for me to find us work and settle. Once I have a place, it'll be easier. We can do what we want. Trust me as you did all those years ago."

"Okay."

He quieted my concerns with more drinking, and I did as he asked, waiting faithfully for the time I could emerge again. A longing to connect with others - not just Mike - had been growing. It'd been good to experience Mike's social success, but he didn't care for friends or girls because he didn't trust anyone, not even me. Maybe me especially.

I wanted more. I couldn't linger until death without feeling something. No matter how broken we are, no one can kill the urge to be loved by someone. I wanted that.

Mike didn't care, and I understood why. He only thought of surviving, coasting through life with his back against the wall and the world ahead. Us and them. No one else. I tried hard to make him understand but it was impossible to convince him that he might be wrong for once.

"I don't think so," he said. "And what's the point? People suck. They'll hurt you."

"Maybe they won't? Maybe we'll find some good ones?"

Mike lost his patience. "I don't know how to tell you, Michael."

"What?"

"Living inside me has stunted your growth. Given the chance, what would you say to someone?"

I had to think about that for too long. The exit within Mike revealed itself again, and another row of serrated anxieties appeared.

"Sorry, kid. You're better off inside."

Despite the logic and the risk and the obvious pain of exit, I continued to debate him until, finally, one evening, another spent at the bar after work as a laborer for a demolition company (a job Mike enjoyed), a woman said hello.

"Hello," I said, and, somehow, the words found their way out of Mike's mouth. Anger made his nostrils flare. He did not approve. She began to ask questions, and I answered because Mike let me.

"You're going to see," he said. "I'm sorry you've chosen to learn this way."

Excited, afraid, I ignored his warning and began to relax.

"I'm Michael."

"Cora."

We talked for half an hour.

"Time for me to go," she said. Mike paid for her and I offered to walk with her when she said which way was home. It wasn't too far from us.

Cora hesitated.

"I understand if you'd rather not," Mike said, and I wondered why he decided to get involved. "I'm near there." And he told her our street. We all left together.

"Thank you, Mike." I felt incredible despite wanting to throw up. The cool night air kept nervous sweat beads from forming on Mike's skin. We walked and chatted a little until the conversation abruptly ceased. Cora looked toward a darkened porch.

"Thought I'd left the lights on," she said.

"Do you think someone turned them off?" I asked.

"No," she said. "I just don't like it. It's so dark out here already."

"Yeah."

She waited.

I waited too.

"Here we go," Mike said to me. I didn't get what he meant. I didn't care. Cora was waiting for something. I figured that meant I had something to do.

"Let me?" I begged Mike.

"It's all you, kid."

I took her hand.

She pulled away as if burned. "Look, I think you should go."

"I don't understand," I said. "We were getting along so well."

"Yes, it was nice talking to you. And nice of you to see me home. But I think you got the wrong idea."

"Wrong idea? I don't understand." She'd been interested. I'd been so sure. We waited some more. I didn't know what to do.

She took her phone from her pocket. "Look, if you don't leave, I'm calling the cops."

"The cops?"

After another silent beat, she began to type away. I didn't know what was happening.

"Mike? Mike? What is she doing?" I was beginning to panic. Mike didn't answer. "Mike! Please!"

His heavy hands seized her wrists so firmly she squealed and dropped the phone. Things went sideways from there. I couldn't retreat fast enough to the interior. Mike dragged her to the house and laughed as she screamed.

"Mike, don't," I pleaded.

"You understand now," he answered. "And now I clean up your mess." He sounded irritated but soon began to enjoy the ordeal, toying with her, making her suffer, making her beg for her life.

Consumed by fear and revulsion, I tried hard to drown in the interior numbness of Mike without success. He either wouldn't let me or couldn't spare me from the unspeakable horror inflicted upon the poor, kind woman in the wrong place at the wrong time.

After he had finished, Mike chuckled. "Admit it, Michael. Part of you found that thrilling."

"No," I told him, my voice so very quiet. "It was wrong. Her only crime was talking to me."

"So you see now why you can't come out?"

"I see."

He went on to explain anyway. "No one can accept you, Michael. No one will ever love you. Or me."

"It's easier for you," I accused him.

"Of course," Mike admitted, "I accepted it a long time ago, back when you only suspected it could be so. I'm sorry, Michael."

"No, you're not."

Mike didn't answer. He turned instead to the broken woman he'd left in the bathtub. "I need to get rid of Cora." He had an idea in mind already and wasn't asking for suggestions. His first taste of flesh was raw and he found it acceptable.

"God, no," I said.

"Quiet now, Michael. I need you to be quiet."

I didn't have the will to reject him.

With some knives from the kitchen, he cut away every fleshy part and tried various methods of preparation. By noon the following day, Mike had two suitcases of messy steaks, blended organs, and bones.

"We won't need to buy meat for a while," he told me. "That's good news, Michael."

"It isn't. We deserve to die."

"Quiet."

He hauled it all home and returned to Cora's later to clean up further. Satisfied no one would suspect foul play at the scene, Mike proceeded to the next stage: Disposal.

Patiently, he grinded bones to powder, and discarded it at work. He hid teeth amongst bread crumbs and tossed them to the ducks at the lake. All of it, he enjoyed like a secret game, and, when I objected, more rows of teeth appeared to prevent and stifle an escape.

"You can't come out," he said. "Look what happened to Cora." He couldn't suppress a giggle.

"You can't come out. The police will put us in jail forever. You think your parents were bad? Let me tell you about the other inmates."

"There's no point in coming out. Nobody wants to see you."

It was hard to argue. Mike was right. Time, I thought, would bring back the lack of feeling I so desperately desired. But then he wanted more.

It started with a long walk. Mike saw them at the park, a family of four. The kids were little. This mom and dad looked so happy to see their children's joy.

That first encounter angered Mike. "Stop crying, Michael. Stop it. It isn't fair, and you know it. Why should those little assholes get everything and you get nothing?"

"It's not how life works. You're trying to convince yourself of something I want no part of. You don't need me to do it, and I don't think you should."

"What the hell do you know about life from in there?" Mike slapped his solid belly. "You hate them too. Admit it."

"I'm jealous. Sure. I wish I'd had what they seem to. It's not hatred. It's different. I think I'd like to get out now." In that total darkness, the vicious exit remained. It always seemed to be there with its false hope. Maybe because I thought more of leaving.

"Just try it," Mike said. "See what happens."

He began to prepare, visiting different hardware stores and a Walmart so that his purchases didn't raise suspicion: Rope, nails, a claw hammer, a set of cooking knives.

"I will skin the youngest alive," he said as he examined his new filet knife.

I couldn't stay silent. "No. Please. Stop."

Mike just smiled. "You know you want to see what happens too."

"I don't. Please, leave them alone."

"I'll tell you what..."

He proposed I write to you anything I wanted.

I thought it best to explain the situation in context, so that you might be moved to help me and, more importantly, the family Mike has targeted for a gruesome end.

If even twelve people object, he swears he won't do it. If enough of you agree, he'll let me out.

Please, save these people.

Free me.

You are my last hope.

You are theirs too.

He says we have till the wrong side of midnight to convince him.

Update: Mike lied.

About the Author

AP Cleriot lives in Ontario, Canada with his wife, daughters, and two hilarious cats. He was a contributor to Cracked.com and other well known websites before switching to horror. Collegiate is his debut spooky novel.

He thanks you for reading this bio, and wishes you well.

Read more at https://linktr.ee/cleriotnoir.